Colin is a schoolfriend of Peter, George and Jack. He and George often work as a pair on the Secret Seven's adventures. He is quieter than Peter or Jack, and usually follows their instructions.

George is at school with Colin, Peter and Jack. He and Colin often work together on the Seven's tasks. He is a helpful member of the Seven, but not a natural leader.

Janet is Peter's sister and together they invented the Secret Seven. Janet is at school with Pam and Barbara, and is the most resourceful and independent of the three girls. Unlike some brothers and sisters, she and Peter get on very well.

Scamper is not a full member of the Secret Seven but he does share in all their adventures. He is Peter and Janet's dog and enjoys guarding the Seven when they have their meetings.

ISBN 0 361 05583 8
Copyright © 1983 Darrell Waters Limited
"Secret Seven on the Trail" first published by Hodder
and Stoughton Limited in 1952
Copyright © 1983 Purnell Publishers Limited as to the artwork
and features herein
Published 1983 by Purnell Books, Paulton, Bristol, BS18 5LQ,
a member of the BPCC group of companies
Made and printed in Italy

Secret Seven on the Trail

''Secret Seven on the Trail'' is an amazing story
of strange happenings as a gang of thieves plan
and carry out a series of daring robberies.
Because of an odd coincidence, only the Secret
Seven can bring the gang to justice and so
begins a tale of excitement and adventure.
As well as Enid Blyton's thrilling story there are
all sorts of quizzes and features related to the
Secret Seven, so there will be hours of fun and
excitement for everyone!

Chapter 1
The Secret Seven Meet

'Mummy, have you got anything we could have to drink?' asked Janet. 'And to eat too?'

'But you've only *just* finished your breakfast!' said Mummy in surprise. 'And you each had two sausages. You can't possibly want anything more yet.'

'Well, we're having the very last meeting of the Secret Seven this morning,' said Janet. 'Down in the shed. We don't think it's worth while meeting when we all go back to school, nothing exciting ever happens then.'

'We're going to meet again when the Christmas holidays come,' said Peter. 'Aren't we, Scamper, old boy?'

The golden spaniel wagged his tail hard, and gave a small bark.

'He says, he hopes he can come to the last meeting too,' said Janet. 'Of course you can, Scamper.'

'He didn't say that,' said Peter, grinning. 'He said that if there were going to be snacks of any kind at this meeting he'd like to join in!'

'Woof,' agreed Scamper, and put his paw up on Peter's knee.

'I'll give you lemons, and some sugar and you can make your own lemonade,' said Mummy. 'You like doing that, don't you? And you can go and see if there are any rock-buns left in the tin in the larder. They'll be stale, but I know you don't mind that!'

'Oh, thanks, Mummy,' said Janet 'Come on, Peter. We'd better get the things now, because the others will be here soon!'

They ran off to the larder, Scamper panting behind. Rock-buns! Stale or not, Scamper liked those as much as the children did.

Janet took some lemons, and went to get the sugar from her mother. Peter emptied the stale rock-buns on to a plate, and the two of them, followed by Scamper, went down to the shed. Janet had the lemon-squeezer and a big jug of water. It was fun to make lemonade.

They pushed open the shed door. On it were the letters S.S. in green—S.S. for the Secret Seven!

'Our Secret Society has been going for some time now,' said Janet, beginning to squeeze a lemon. 'I'm not a bit tired of it, are you, Peter?'

'Good gracious, no!' said Peter. 'Why, think of all the adventures we've had, and the exciting things we've done! But

I do think it's sensible not to bother about the Secret Seven meetings till the hols. For one thing, in this Christmas term the days get dark very quickly, and we have to be indoors.'

'Yes, and nothing much happens then,' said Janet. 'Oh, Scamper—you won't like that squeezed out lemon-skin, you silly dog! Drop it!'

Scamper dropped it. He certainly didn't like it! He sat with his tongue hanging out, looking most disgusted. Peter glanced at his watch.

'Nearly time for the others to come,' he said. 'I hope they'll agree to this being the last meeting till Christmas. We'd better collect all the badges from them, and put them in a safe place. If we don't, someone is bound to lose one.'

'Or that silly sister of Jack's will take it and wear it herself,' said Janet. 'What's her name—Susie? Aren't you glad I'm not annoying to you, like Susie is to Jack, Peter?'

'Well, you're pretty annoying sometimes,' said Peter, and immediately got a squirt of lemon-juice in his eye from an angry Janet! 'Oh, don't do that. Don't you know that lemon-juice smarts like anything? Stop it, Janet!'

Janet stopped it. 'I'd better not waste the juice,' she said. 'Ah, here comes someone.'

Scamper barked as somebody walked up the path and rapped on the door.

'Password!' called Peter, who never opened the door to anyone until the correct password was called.

'Pickled onions!' said a voice, and giggled.

That was the latest password of the Secret Seven, suggested by Colin, whose mother had been pickling onions on the day of the last meeting they had had. It was such a silly password that everyone had laughed, and Peter had said they would have it till they thought of a better one.

'Got your badge?' said Peter, opening the door.

Outside stood Barbara. She displayed her badge proudly. 'It's a new one,' she said. 'My old one's got so dirty, so I made this.'

'Very good,' said Peter. 'Come in. Look, here come three others.'

He shut the door again, and Barbara sat down on a box beside Janet, and watched her stirring the lemonade. Rat-a-tat! Scamper barked as knocking came at the door again.

'Password!' called out Peter, Janet and Barbara together.

'Pickled onions!' yelled back everyone. Peter flung open the door and scowled.

'How MANY times am I to tell you not to yell out the password!' he said. 'Now everyone in hearing distance has heard it.'

'Well, you all yelled out PASSWORD at the tops of your voices,' said Jack. 'Anyway, we can easily choose a new one.' He looked slyly at George, who had come in with him. 'George thought it was pickled cabbage, and we had to tell him it wasn't.'

'Well, of all the—' began Peter, but just then another knock came on the door and Scamper growled.

'Password!' called Peter.

'Pickled onions!' came his mother's voice, and she laughed. 'If that *is* a password! I've brought you some home-made peppermints, just to help the last meeting along.'

'Oh. Thanks, Mummy,' said Janet, and opened the door. She took the peppermints and gave them to Peter. Peter frowned round, when his mother had gone.

'There you are, you see,' he said. 'It just happened to be my mother who heard the password, but it might have been anybody. Now who's still missing?'

'There's me here, and you, George, Jack, Barbara and Pam,' said Janet. 'Colin's missing. Oh, here he comes.'

Rat-tat! Scamper gave a little welcoming bark. He knew every S.S. member quite well. Colin gave the password and was admitted. Now the Secret Seven were complete.

'Good,' said Peter. 'Sit down, Colin. We'll get down to business as soon as Janet pours out the lemonade. Buck up, Janet!'

Chapter 2
No more meetings till Christmas

JANET poured out mugs of the lemonade, and Peter handed round the rock-buns.

'A bit stale,' he said, 'but nice and curranty. Two each and one for old Scamper. Sorry, Scamper; but, after all, you're not a *real* member of the Secret Seven, or you could have two.'

'He couldn't,' said Jack. 'There are only fifteen buns. And anyway, I *always* count him as a real member.'

'You can't. We're the Secret *Seven*, and Scamper makes eight,' said Peter. 'But he can always come with us. Now listen, this is to be the last meeting, and—'

There were surprised cries at once.

'The *last* meeting! Why, what's happening?'

'The *last* one! Surely you're not going to stop the Secret Seven?'

'Oh but, Peter—surely you're not meaning—'

'Just let me *speak*,' said Peter. 'It's to be the last meeting till the holidays come again. Tomorrow all of us boys go back to school, and the girls go to their school the day after. Nothing ever happens in term-time, and anyway we're too busy to look for adventure, so—'

'But something *might* happen,' said Colin. 'You just never know. I think it's a silly idea to stop the Secret Seven for the term-time. I do really.'

'So do I,' said Pam. 'I like belonging to it, and wearing my badge, and remembering the password.'

'Well, you can still wear your badges if you like,' said Peter, 'though I *had* thought of collecting them today, as we're all wearing them, and keeping them till our meeting next hols.'

'I'm not giving *mine* up,' said Jack, firmly. 'And you needn't be afraid I'll let my sister Susie get it, either, because I've got a perfectly good hiding-place for it.'

'And suppose, just *suppose*, something turned up in term-time,' said Colin, earnestly. 'Suppose one of us happened on something queer, something that ought to be looked into. What would we do if the Secret Seven was disbanded till Christmas?'

'Nothing ever turns up in termtime,' repeated Peter, who liked getting his own way. 'And anyway I've got to work jolly hard this term. My father wasn't at all keen on my last report.'

'All right. You work hard, and keep out of the Society till Christmas,' said Jack. 'I'll run it with Janet. It can be the Secret Six till then. S.S. will stand for that as much as for Secret Seven.'

That didn't please Peter at all. He frowned. 'No,' he said. 'I'm the head. But seeing that you all seem to disagree with me, I'll say this. We won't have any *regular* meetings, like we have been having, but only call one if anything

does happen to turn up. And you'll see I'm right. Nothing will happen!'

'We keep our badges, then, and have a password?' said Colin. 'We're still a very live Society, even if nothing happens? And we call a meeting at once if something does!'

'Yes,' said everyone, looking at Peter. They loved being the Secret Seven. It made them feel important, even if, as Colin said, nothing happened for them to look into.

'All right,' said Peter. 'What about a new password?'

Everyone thought hard. Jack looked at Scamper, who seemed to be thinking too. 'What about Scamper's name?' he said. '"Scamper" would be a good password.'

'It wouldn't,' said Janet. 'Every time anyone gave the password Scamper would think he was being called!'

'Let's have *my* dog's name—Rover,' said Pam.

'No, have my aunt's dogs name,' said Jack. 'Cheeky Charlie. That's a good password.'

'Yes! Cheeky Charlie! We'll have

that,' said Peter. 'Nobody would ever think of that for a password. Right— Cheeky Charlie it is!'

The rock-buns were passed round for the second time. Scamper eyed them longingly. He had had his. Pam took pity on him and gave him half hers, and Barbara did the same.

Scamper then fixed his eyes mournfully on Jack, who quickly gave him a large piece of his bun too.

'Well!' said Peter. 'Scamper's had more than any real member of the Secret Seven! He'll be thinking he can run the whole Society soon!'

'Wuff,' said Scamper, thumping his tail on the ground, and looking at Peter's bun.

The lemonade was finished. The last crumb of cake had been licked up by Scamper. The sun came out and shone down through the shed window.

'Come on, let's go out and play,' said Peter, getting up. 'School tomorrow! Well, these have been jolly good hols. Now, Secret Seven, you all know the password, don't you? You probably won't have to use it till the Christmas holidays, so just make up your minds to remember it.'

The Famous Secret Seven
Rock Buns

These are probably Scamper's favourites, as you will know when you read 'Secret Seven On The Trail', but the making of them is something that even the cleverest of golden spaniels cannot manage! With a little care and, for safety's sake, a watchful grown-up, YOU can! Though delicious they are really quite simple.

YOU WILL NEED:
200g or 8oz of self-raising flour.
100g or 4oz butter.
75g or 3oz caster sugar.
100g or 4oz mixed dried fruit.
1 standard egg, beaten.
2 to 4 teaspoons of milk.
These amounts are enough for roughly 10 buns.

METHOD:

1 Sift the flour into a bowl and add the butter, which is cut into small pieces.

2 Rub the butter and flour between your fingertips until the mixture resembles fine bread-crumbs.

3 Stir in the sugar and fruit.

4 Make a hollow in the centre and add the beaten egg and the milk. Thoroughly mix until you have a very stiff batter.

5 Now, grease a baking tray with some more butter and place small spoonfuls (10 in all) of your stiff mixture onto the tray, carefully making little rocky mounds. Since they will spread slightly, allow some room between each bun.

6 This is the moment when the grown-up watches closely, for you will need your oven heated to 200°C or 400°F. This is moderately hot.

7 Place the tray just above the centre of the oven and bake for 15 to 20 minutes. Afterwards allow to cool on a wire rack. Then enjoy a super meal with your Secret Seven rock buns!

Chapter 3
The Famous Five

THE BOYS AND GIRLS RETURNED TO THEIR SEPARATE SCHOOLS, BUT THEY ALL WORE THEIR SECRET SEVEN BADGES, AND IT WAS FUN TO SEE THE OTHER CHILDREN LOOKING ENVIOUSLY AT THEM..

GO ON, LET US JOIN—WHY CAN'T YOU?

NO, YOU CAN'T. IT'S A **SECRET** SOCIETY. I'M NOT SUPPOSED EVEN TO TALK ABOUT IT.

I DON'T SEE WHY YOU CAN'T MAKE IT A BIT BIGGER AND LET **US** COME IN.

YOU CAN'T HAVE MORE THAN SEVEN IN OUR SOCIETY, AND WE'VE GOT SEVEN. YOU GO AND MAKE SECRET SOCIETIES OF YOUR OWN!

That was an unfortunate thing to say! Kate and Susie, who was Jack's tiresome sister, immediately went off to make a society of their own! How very annoying! They got Harry, Jeff and Sam as well as themselves. Five of them, and then, to the intense annoyance of the Secret Seven, these five appeared at school with badges of their own!

IT MEANS 'FAMOUS FIVE'! WE'VE NAMED OURSELVES AFTER THE 'FAMOUS FIVE' IN THE 'FIVE' BOOKS. **MUCH** BETTER IDEA THAN THE 'SECRET SEVEN'.

AND AT HOME

WE'VE GOT A GOOD SOCIETY. OUR BADGES ARE BIGGER, WE'VE GOT A SPLENDID PASS-WORD, AND WE HAVE A SECRET SIGN, TOO. **YOU** HAVEN'T GOT THAT!

WHAT'S YOUR SECRET SIGN? **I'VE** NEVER SEEN YOU MAKE IT.

OF COURSE NOT. I TELL YOU IT'S A **SECRET** ONE!

AND WE'RE MEETING EVERY SATURDAY MORNING. AND, WHAT'S MORE, WE'VE GOT AN ADVENTURE GOING ALREADY.

I DON'T BELIEVE YOU. ANYWAY YOU'RE JUST A COPY-CAT. IT WAS **OUR** IDEA!

WELL, YOU WOULDN'T LET ME BELONG TO YOUR SILLY SECRET SEVEN. NOW I BELONG TO THE FAMOUS FIVE, AND I TELL YOU, WE'VE GOT AN ADVENTURE ALREADY!

JACK DIDN'T KNOW WHETHER TO BELIEVE SUSIE OR NOT...

DON'T TAKE ANY NOTICE OF HER. FAMOUS FIVE INDEED! THEY'LL SOON GET TIRED OF MEETING AND PLAYING ABOUT!

THE FAMOUS FIVE SOCIETY WAS VERY ANNOYING TO THE SECRET SEVEN THAT TERM. THE MEMBERS WORE THEIR BADGES EVERY DAY. KATE AND SUSIE TALKED IN EXCITED WHISPERS, AS IF SOMETHING REALLY **WAS** HAPPENING.

HARRY, JEFF AND SAM DID THE SAME AT THEIR SCHOOL, WHICH ANNOYED PETER, COLIN, JACK AND GEORGE VERY MUCH.

THE FIVE MET IN THE SUMMER-HOUSE IN JACK'S GARDEN, AND SUSIE ACTUALLY ORDERED JACK TO KEEP OUT...

AS IF I SHALL KEEP OUT OF MY OWN GARDEN! I BELIEVE THEY REALLY **HAVE** GOT HOLD OF SOMETHING. I THINK SOMETHING **IS** UP!

WOULDN'T IT BE AWFUL IF **THEY** HAD AN ADVENTURE AND WE DIDN'T? SUSIE WOULD CROW LIKE ANYTHING.

IT'S UP TO YOU TO FIND OUT ABOUT IT, JACK. TRY AND FIND OUT WHAT'S UP— WE'LL SOON PUT A STOP TO IT.

SO, NEXT SATURDAY MORNING, WHEN THE FAMOUS FIVE WERE DUE TO MEET AGAIN, JACK HID BEHIND THE SUMMER-HOUSE. UNFORTUNATELY, HE DIDN'T KNOW HE'D BEEN SPOTTED...

AH-HAH...

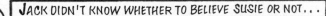

17

SUSIE RAN DOWNSTAIRS TO MEET THE OTHERS.....

JACK'S GOING TO TRY AND FIND OUT WHAT WE'RE DOING. HE'S HIDING AT THE BACK OF THE SUMMER HOUSE TO LISTEN TO WHAT WE SAY!

I'LL GO AND PULL HIM OUT!

NO! I'VE GOT A BETTER IDEA. LET'S GO TO THE SUMMER-HOUSE, WHISPER THE PASSWORD AND THEN TALK AS THOUGH WE REALLY **HAD** FOUND AN ADVENTURE!

BUT WHY?

BECAUSE JACK WILL BELIEVE IT. AND IF WE MENTION THAT OLD HOUSE ON THE HILL, TIGGER'S BARN, HE'LL TELL THE SECRET SEVEN, AND—

AND THEY'LL GO AND INVESTIGATE AND FIND THERE'S NOTHING THERE!

YES. AND WE'LL MENTION STUMPY DICK, AND TWISTY TOM, AND MAKE JACK THINK WE'RE RIGHT IN THE MIDDLE OF SOMETHING!

AND WE'LL GO TO TIGGER'S BARN OURSELVES AND WAIT TILL THEY COME OUT AND HAVE A GOOD LAUGH AT THEM.

COME ON! LET'S GO DOWN TO THE SUMMER-HOUSE NOW, SUSIE. JACK WILL BE WONDERING WHY WE'RE SO LATE.

I'LL GO FIRST, AND YOU CAN ALL COME ONE BY ONE. AND DON'T FORGET TO WHISPER THE PASSWORD, BECAUSE HE MUSTN'T HEAR **THAT!**

SUSIE SPED DOWN TO THE GARDEN AND INTO THE SUMMER-HOUSE. SHE WAS GOING TO HAVE A FINE REVENGE FOR KEEPING HER OUT OF **HIS** SECRET SOCIETY...

Chapter 4
Susie tells a tale

Susie led the talking. She was a good talker, and was determined to puzzle Jack as much as she could.

'I've found out where those rogues are meeting,' she said. 'It's an important piece of news, so please listen. I've tracked them down at last!'

Jack could hardly believe his ears. He listened hard.

'Tell us, Susie,' said Harry, playing up well.

'It's at Tigger's Barn,' said Susie, enjoying herself. 'That old, deserted house up on the hill. A tumbledown old place, just right for rogues to meet in. Far away from anywhere.'

'Oh yes. I know it,' said Jeff.

'Well, Stumpy Dick and Twisty Tom will both be there,' said Susie.

There were 'oooohs' and 'ahs' from her listeners, and Jack very nearly said 'Ooooh' too. Stumpy Dick and Twisty Tom—good gracious! What *had* the Famous Five got on to?

'They're planning something we must find out about,' said Susie, raising her voice a little, to make sure that Jack could hear. 'And we've simply *got* to do something. So one or two of us must go to Tigger's Barn at the right time and hide ourselves.'

'I'll go with you, Susie,' said Jeff at once.

Jack felt surprised when he heard

that. Jeff was a very timid boy, and not at all likely to go and hide in a deserted place like Tigger's Barn. He listened hard.

'All right. You and I will go together,' said Susie. 'It will be dangerous, but what do we care for that? We are the Famous Five!'

'Hurrah!' said Kate and Sam.

'When do we go?' said Jeff.

'Well,' said Susie, 'I *think* they will meet there on Tuesday night. Can you come with me then, Jeff?'

'Certainly,' said Jeff, who would never have *dreamed* of going to Tigger's Barn at night if Susie's tale had been true.

Jack, out in the bush, felt more and more surprised. He also felt a great respect for the Famous Five. My word! They were as good as the Secret Seven! Fancy their getting on to an adventure like this! What a good thing he had managed to hide and hear about it!

He longed to go to Peter and tell him all he had heard. He wondered how his sister Susie knew anything about this affair. Blow Susie! It was just like her to make a Secret Society and then find an adventure for it.

'Suppose Stumpy Dick discovers you?' said Kate.

'I shall knock him to the ground,' said Jeff in a very valiant voice.

This was going a bit too far. Not even the Famous Five could imagine Jeff facing up to anyone. Kate gave a sudden giggle.

That set Sam off, and he gave one of his extraordinary snorts. Susie frowned. If the meeting began to giggle and snort like this, Jack would certainly know it wasn't serious. That would never do.

She frowned heavily at the others. 'Shut up!' she whispered. 'If we begin to giggle Jack won't believe a word.'

'I c-c-can't help it,' said Kate, who never could stop giggling once she began. 'Oh, Sam, please don't snort again!'

'Sh!' said Susie, angrily. 'Don't spoil it all.' Then she raised her voice again so that Jack could hear. 'Well, Famous Five, that's all for today. Meet again when you get your orders, and remember, don't say a word to ANYONE about Tigger's Barn. This is OUR adventure!'

'I bet the Secret Seven wish they could hear about this,' said Jeff, in a loud

voice. 'It makes me laugh to think they don't know anything.'

He laughed, and that was the signal for everyone to let themselves go. Kate giggled again, Sam snorted, Susie roared, and so did Harry. They all thought of Jack out in the laurel bush, drinking in every word of their ridiculous story, and then they laughed all the more. Jack listened crossly. How dare they laugh at the Secret Seven like that?

'Come on,' said Susie, at last. 'This meeting is over. Let's go and get a ball and have a game. I wonder where Jack is? He might like to play too.'

As they all knew quite well where Jack was, this made them laugh again, and they went up the garden path in a very good temper. What a joke to play on a member of the Secret Seven! Would he rush off at once and call a meeting?

Would the Secret Seven go to Tigger's Barn on Tuesday night in the dark?

'Susie, you don't *really* mean to go up to Tigger's Barn on Tuesday night, do you?' said Jeff, as they went up the path.

'Well, I did think of it at first,' said Susie. 'But it would be silly to. It's a long way, and it's dark at night now, and anyway, the Secret Seven might not go, and it would be awfully silly for any of us to go and hide there for nothing!'

'Yes, it would,' said Jeff, much relieved. 'But you'll be able to see if Jack does, won't you, Susie? If he slips off somewhere on Tuesday night, won't we have a laugh!'

'We certainly will!' said Susie. 'Oh, I *do* hope he does! I'll tell him it was all a trick, when he comes back, and won't he be FURIOUS!'

The Secret Seven
NATURE QUIZ

1 How did the Dandelion get its name? (Yes, it really does have a link with the 'King of the Jungle'!)

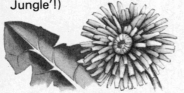

2 How did the ordinary daisy come to be named, and why is it also called 'black-eyed Susan'?

3 To find a four-leafed clover is supposed to be particularly lucky, yet why is the clover plant good fortune for all of us?

4 What is the tallest garden flower you can think of and how high does it quite commonly grow?

5 Which family of plants is completely without any green parts or leaves?

6 Which plant can be used as a compass?

7 What is 'rootstock'?

8 How do trees record their age (except in the tropics)?

9 What is the sweetest and stickiest tree food for humans?

10 What causes knotholes and knots in the trunks of trees and how does it link with pruning?

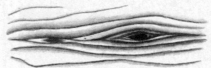

11 What is the purpose of any plant's (or tree's) leaves?

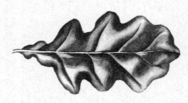

12 Why are certain flowers perfumed and why do others give out ultraviolet rays?

13 How is pollen carried from plant to plant and why is the carrying of pollen so important?

14 Which family of flowers is the favourite of the butterfly?

15 Which family of flowers is the most popular in the world, and how many varieties (roughly) are there?

16 How can you tell the difference between a shrub and a tree, remembering that size is not always the main difference?

17 What shrubs commonly found wild belong to the same family as the Pea and Sweet Pea? Picture the 'winged' flowers of the Sweet Pea and think hard!

18 Which are the oldest and largest trees in the world and how did they gain their unusual name?

19 Did you know you can grow your own miniature forest?

20 In which countries did the Horse-Chestnut originate and when was it first introduced into England?

21 What is a 'Katydid' and how does it make its cheery 'music'?

22 Which insect is able to make paper?

23 Which quite harmless insect, because of old legends, is still sometimes called 'The Devil's Darning Needle'?

24 Why doesn't a spider become entangled in its own sticky web?

25 Which insect is able to make its own parachute and sometimes almost seems to be flying?

26 What is the main difference between a butterfly and a moth?

27 Which popular little insect, a favourite with children, is the friend of all fruit-growers, and why?

28 Since a tortoise has no teeth, how does it tear its food to pieces? It cannot chew!

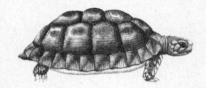

29 Is an eel a true fish, or is it related to the snake?

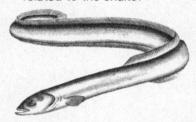

30 Which fish can live out of water for several days and even WALK on land?

31 Which is our smallest bird? Is it rare or just very shy of people?

32 Which famous songbird can be heard clearly at night, and does it also sing during the day?

33 What good news is signalled by the first arrival of swallows?

34 Which popular little bird, perhaps the best known of any, is really amazingly fierce, his song often a battle-cry to warn off others from entering his territory?

35 Why is a female blackbird so often mistaken for a thrush?

36 How does the missel thrush get its name and why is it also sometimes known as a storm-cock?

37 To what main family of birds does the raven belong and why will you always find ravens at the Tower of London?

38 How long has a raven been known to live?

39 In olden days why were ravens always found in London's streets and why were they protected?

40 Which bird, common to almost every garden, is an excellent mimic, not only of other birds' calls but also of a bicycle-pump squeaking or a telephone bell ringing?

Answers on page 77

Chapter 5
Jack tells the news

JACK crept carefully out of the laurel bush as soon as he felt sure that the others were safely out of the way. He dusted himself down and looked round. Nobody was in sight.

He debated with himself what to do. Was it important enough to call a meeting of the Secret Seven? No—he would go and find Peter and tell him first. Peter could decide whether to have a meeting or not.

On the way to Peter's house Jack met George. 'Hallo!' said George, 'you look very solemn! What's up? Have you had a row at home or something?'

'No,' said Jack. 'But I've just found out that the Famous Five are in the middle of something. I heard Susie telling them, down in our summer-house. I was in the laurel bush outside.'

'Is it important?' asked George. 'I mean, your sister Susie's a bit of a nuisance, isn't she? You don't want to pay too much attention to her. She's conceited enough already.'

'Yes, I know,' said Jack. 'But she's clever, you know. And after all, *we* managed to get into a good many adventures, didn't we? And there's really no reason why the Famous Five shouldn't, too, if they keep their eyes and ears open. Listen, and I'll tell you what I heard.'

He told George, and George was most impressed. 'Tigger's Barn!' he said. 'Well, that *would* be a good meeting-place for rogues who wanted to meet without being seen. But how did Susie get hold of the names of the men? I say, Jack, it would be absolutely *maddening* if the Famous Five hit on something important before we did!'

'That's what *I* think,' said Jack. 'Especially as Susie's the ring-leader. She's always trying to boss me, and she would be worse than ever if her silly Society discovered some gang or plot. Let's find Peter, shall we? I was on the way to him when I met you.'

'I'll go with you, then,' said George.

'I'm sure Peter will think it's important. Come on!'

So two solemn boys walked up the path to Peter's house, and went round the back to find him. He was chopping up firewood, one of his Saturday morning jobs. He was very pleased to see Jack and George.

'Oh, hallo,' he said, putting down his chopper. 'Now I can knock off for a bit. Chopping wood is fine for about five minutes, but an awful bore after that. My mother doesn't like me to do it, because she thinks I'll chop my fingers off, but Dad's hard-hearted and makes me do it each Saturday.'

'Peter,' said Jack, 'I've got some news.'

'Oh, what?' asked Peter. 'Tell me.'

So Jack told him about how he had hidden in the laurel bush and overheard a meeting of the Famous Five. 'They've got a password, of course,' he said, 'but I couldn't hear it. However, they forgot to whisper once they had said the password, and I heard every word.'

He told Peter what he had heard, but Peter didn't take it seriously. He was most annoying.

He listened to the end, and then he threw back his head and laughed. 'Oh Jack! Surely you didn't fall for all that nonsense? Susie must have been pretending. I expect that's what they do at their silly meetings—pretend they are in the middle of an adventure, and kid themselves they're clever.'

'But it all sounded absolutely serious,' said Jack, beginning to feel annoyed. 'I mean, they had no idea I was listening, they all seemed quite serious. And Jeff was ready to go and investigate on Tuesday evening!'

'What, *Jeff! Can* you imagine that little coward of a Jeff going to look for a *mouse*, let alone Stumpy Dick and the other fellow, whatever his name is!' said

Peter, laughing again. 'He'd run a mile before he'd go to Tigger's Barn at night. That sister of yours was just putting up a bit of make-believe, Jack, silly kid's stuff, like pretending to play at Red Indians or something, that's all.'

'Then you don't think it's worth while calling a meeting of the Secret Seven and asking some of us to go to Tigger's Barn on Tusday night?' said Jack, in a hurt voice.

'No, I don't,' said Peter. 'I'm not such a fathead as to believe in Susie's fairy-tales.'

'But suppose the Famous Five go, and discover something *we* ought to discover?' said George.

'Well, if Jack sees Susie and Jeff creeping off somewhere on Tuesday evening, he can follow them,' said Peter, still grinning. 'But they won't go! You'll see I'm right. It's all make-believe!'

'All right,' said Jack, getting up. 'If that's what you think there's no use in talking about it any longer. But you'll be sorry if you find you ought to have called a meeting and didn't, Peter! Susie may be a nuisance, but she's jolly clever, *too* clever, and I wouldn't be a bit surprised if the Famous Five weren't beginning an adventure *we* ought to have!'

Peter began to chop wood again, still smiling in a most superior way. Jack marched off, his head in the air, very cross. George went with him. They said nothing for a little while, and then George looked doubtfully at Jack.

'Peter's very certain about it all, isn't he?' he said. 'Do you think he's right? After all, he's the chief of the Secret Seven. We ought to obey.'

'Look here, George. I'm going to wait and see what Susie does on Tuesday evening,' said Jack. 'If she stays at home, I'll know Peter's right, and it's all make-believe on her part. But if she goes off by herself, or Jeff comes to call for her, I'll know there's something up, and I'll follow them!'

'That's a good idea,' said George. 'I'll come with you, if you like.'

'I shan't know what time they'll go, though, if they *do* go,' said Jack. 'I know, you come to tea with me on Tuesday, George. Then we can follow Susie and Jeff at once, if they slip off. And if they don't go out, then we'll know it's nonsense and I'll apologize to Peter the next morning for being such a fathead.'

'Right,' said George, pleased. 'I'll come to tea on Tuesday, then, and we'll keep a close watch on Susie. I'm glad I haven't got a sister like that! You never know what she's up to!'

When Jack got home, he went straight to his mother. 'Mother,' he said, 'may I have George to tea on Tuesday, please?'

Susie was there, reading in a corner. She pricked up her ears at once, and grinned in delight. She guessed that Jack and George meant to follow her and Jeff—if they went! All right, she would take the joke a little farther.

'Oh, that reminds me, Mother,' she said. 'Could I have *Jeff* to tea on Tuesday too? It's rather important! I can? Thank you very much!'

Chapter 6
Susie's little trick

Jack was pleased when he heard Susie asking for Jeff to come to tea on Tuesday.

'That just proves it!' he said to himself. 'They will slip off to Tigger's Barn together. Peter was quite wrong! Let me see. Tuesday is the evening Mother goes to a Committee Meeting, so Susie and Jeff can go off without anyone bothering. And so can I! Aha! George and I will be on their track all right.'

Jack told George, who agreed that it did look as if there really was something in all that had been said at the meeting of the Famous Five.

'We'll keep a jolly good watch on Susie and Jeff, and follow them at once,' said George. 'They'll be most annoyed to find

we are with them in Tigger's Barn! We'd better take a torch, Jack. It will be dark.'

'Not awfully dark,' said Jack. 'There will be a moon. But it might be cloudy so we certainly will take a torch.'

Susie told Jeff, with many giggles, that Jack had asked George to tea on Tuesday. 'So I've asked for you to come too,' she said. 'And after tea, Jeff, you and I will slip out secretly, and make Jack and George think we are off to Tigger's Barn, but really and truly we will only be hiding somewhere, and we'll go back and play as soon as we are certain Jack and George have gone off to try and follow us to Tigger's Barn! Oh, dear, they'll go all the way there, and won't find a thing, except a horrid old tumbledown house!'

'It serves them right!' said Jeff. 'All I can say is that I'm jolly glad *I'm* not going off to that lonely place at night.'

Tuesday afternoon came, and with it came Jeff and George after school, on their way to tea with Jack and Susie. The two boys walked with Jack, who pretended to be astonished that Jeff should go to tea with Susie.

'Going to play with her dolls?' he asked. 'Or perhaps you're going to spring-clean the dolls' house?'

Jeff went red. 'Don't be a fathead,' he said. 'I've got my new railway set with me. We're going to play with that.'

'But it takes ages to set out on the floor,' said Jack, surprised.

'Well, what of it?' said Jeff, scowling. Then he remembered that Jack and George thought that he and Susie were going off to Tigger's Barn, and would naturally imagine that he wouldn't have time to play such a lengthy game as trains. He grinned to himself. Let Jack be puzzled! It would do him good!

They all had a very good tea, and then went to the playroom upstairs. Jeff began to set out his railway lines. Jack and George would have liked to help, but they were afraid that Susie might point out that Jeff was *her* guest, not theirs. Susie had a very sharp tongue when she liked!

So they contented themselves with trying to make a rather complicated model aeroplane, keeping a sharp eye on Susie and Jeff all the time.

Very soon Jack's mother put her head in at the door. 'Well, I'm off to my Committee Meeting,' she said. 'You must both go home at eight o'clock, Jeff and George—and Jack, if I'm not back in time for your supper, make yourself something, and then go and have your baths.'

'Right, Mother,' said Jack. 'Come and say good-night to us when you get back.'

As soon as her mother had gone, Susie went all mysterious. She winked at Jeff, who winked back. Jack saw the winks, of course. They meant him to! He was on the alert at once. Ah, those two were probably going to slip out into the night!

'Jeff, come and see the new clock we've got downstairs,' said Susie. 'It has a little man who comes out at the top

30

and strikes a hammer on an anvil to mark every quarter of an hour. It is nearly a quarter past seven, let's go and watch him come out.'

'Right,' said Jeff, and the two went out, nudging each other, and laughing.

'There they go,' said George. 'Do we follow them straightaway?'

Jack went to the door. 'They've gone downstairs,' he said. 'They will get their coats out of the hall cupboard. We'll give them a minute to put them on, then we'll get ours. We shall hear the front door bang, I expect. It won't take us a minute to follow them.'

In about a minute they heard the front door being opened, and then it shut rather quietly, as if it was not really meant to be heard.

'Did you hear that?' asked Jack. 'They shut it very quietly. Come on, we'll pull on our coats and follow. We don't want to track them too closely, or they'll see us. We will jolly well surprise them when they get to Tigger's Barn, though!'

They put on their coats, and opened the front foor. It was fairly light outside because of the rising moon. They took a torch with them, in case the clouds became thick.

There was no sign of Jeff and Susie.

'They have gone at top speed, I should think!' said Jack, closing the door behind him. 'Come on, we know the way to Tigger's Barn, even if we don't spot Jeff and Susie in front of us.'

They went down the garden path. They did not hear the giggles that followed them! Jeff and Susie were hiding behind the big hall curtains, and were now watching Jack and George going down the path. They clutched one another as they laughed. What a fine joke they had played on the two boys!

31

The Mouse Ran up the Clock

He must have been a very clever mouse! For it's not as easy as you may think to recognise a true clock, or be able to tell someone what it does.

Really a clock is a time-telling instrument in which some kind of stored energy, such as a spring or a weight, drives a hand or hands round a dial. So shadow clocks, sundials and sand-filled hourglasses do not really count, though they are amongst the earliest time-measurers known.

In England the making of truly mechanical clocks began in 1386 when three craftsmen from Delft in

Holland were granted special permission and facilities by Edward III to set up business here. The earliest clocks were very large, being made for monasteries, cathedrals and other important buildings. Later, as they were skilfully made smaller and more portable, they began to be used in the ordinary homes of the wealthy. A very famous and early example of a 'public' clock is the one at Dover Castle, though similar turret clocks at Salisbury and Wells Cathedrals are probably older.

In the different Royal Palaces are a number of Crown Clocks, most of them great works of art and the finest examples of the clock-maker's skill. Perhaps the most romantic is the one given by Henry VIII as his wedding present to the ill-fated Anne Boleyn. It measures only four inches by ten inches and is beautifully decorated with 'lovers' knots', and was finally bought by Queen Victoria for the sum of £110 5 shillings!

At Windsor Castle is another very famous kind of clock known as an 'Act of Parliament Clock', being manufactured on account of a tax on all watches imposed by the then Prime Minister Pitt. This caused watches to be worn less and less, so inn-keepers bought the boldy designed 'Act of Parliament Clocks' in order to help out their customers.

Another very unusual and beautiful clock is at Buckingham Palace and is set in a Negress Head case, made of ormulu. Standing over two feet high, it shows the hours in her twinkling eyes, its French spring balance being made by the famous Lepine.

Of course any mention of clocks must include the world-renowned Big Ben, remembering that 'Big Ben' is really the name of its bell (amusingly, a cracked bell at that!). After many misfortunes it was started in 1856 and named after Sir Benjamin Hall who was first Commissioner of Works. The pendulum is so finely balanced that even the addition of the tiniest of weights would badly throw out the timekeeping.

Today there are clocks which hardly resemble ordinary ones at all, such as atomic clocks. They are the most accurate in the world. Their name has nothing to do with atomic power but rather to the natural properties of the atom. Their time-keeping is quite incredible and can only be checked by the most complex of instruments and calculations. The National Physics Laboratory is where one may be found; others are at Greenwich and New York.

Chapter 7
At Tigger's Barn

THEY HURRIED OFF TOWARDS TIGGER'S BARN, BUT COULDN'T UNDERSTAND WHY SUSIE AND JEFF WERE NOT TO BE SEEN...

THEY MUST HAVE TAKEN BICYCLES. THEY **COULDN'T** HAVE GONE SO QUICKLY. HAS SUSIE A BIKE, JACK?

OH, YES, AND I BET SHE'S LENT JEFF MINE.

THEY'LL BE AT TIGGER'S BARN AGES BEFORE US. I HOPE THE MEETING OF THOSE MEN ISN'T OVER BEFORE WE GET THERE.

WE DON'T WANT SUSIE AND JEFF TO HEAR EVERYTHING WITHOUT US HEARING IT, TOO!

DO YOU REMEMBER WHEN WE EXPLORED THE OLD BARN WITH PETER, JACK?

The two boys held their breath. Good gracious! They were right in the middle of something very queer! Why were these men meeting at this tumbledown place? Who were they and what were they doing? Where were Susie and Jeff, too? Were they listening and watching as well?

YES! THERE WAS AN OLD TRAMP ASLEEP IN A CORNER, AND HE ROSE UP AND SHOUTED AT US SO LOUDLY THAT WE ALL RAN AWAY! I'M NOT LIKELY TO FORGET THAT!

THEY TRUDGED ON...

WALK QUIETLY — WE DON'T WANT TO LET JEFF AND SUSIE KNOW WE'RE HERE.

OR THOSE MEN EITHER! BUT ALL IS QUIET. I DON'T THINK THE MEN ARE HERE.

THE BOYS CREPT TO THE BACK OF THE OLD HOUSE...

THEY ENTERED THE HOUSE BY A DOWNSTAIRS WINDOW...

AND THEN A SCUTTLING NOISE MADE JACK JUMP!

WHAT'S THAT?

DON'T GRAB ME LIKE THAT! IT WAS ONLY A RAT! YOU NEARLY MADE ME YELL WHEN YOU GRABBED ME!

LISTEN! SOMETHING'S MOVING HIGH UP IN THAT CHIMNEY!

PROBABLY JUST THE OWL. YES, LISTEN TO IT HOOTING!

SH! WHAT'S THAT NOISE?

A QUAVERING HOOT CAME TO THEIR EARS—BUT IT SEEMED TO COME FROM OUTSIDE...

THAT'S NOT AN OWL. IT'S MEN SIGNALLING TO ONE ANOTHER. THEY **ARE** MEETING HERE! BUT WHERE ARE SUSIE AND JEFF?

HIDDEN SAFELY SOMEWHERE, I EXPECT. WE'D BETTER HIDE TOO. THOSE MEN WILL BE HERE IN HALF A MINUTE.

THERE'S A GOOD HIDING PLACE IN THE HEARTH. WE CAN STAND THERE IN DARKNESS. COME ON, QUICK. I'M SURE I CAN HEAR FOOTSTEPS OUTSIDE.

THE TWO BOYS RAN SILENTLY TO THE HEARTH, ANKLE DEEP IN ASHES...

NEXT MOMENT...

THEN...

COME ON IN. NOBODY'S HERE. LARRY HASN'T COME YET. GIVE HIM THE SIGNAL, ZEB, IN CASE HE'S WAITING ABOUT FOR IT NOW.

FROM THEIR HIDING-PLACE THE BOYS HEARD SOMEONE GIVE A QUAVERING HOOT AGAIN — THEN AN ANSWERING CALL CAME FROM SOME WAY AWAY...

The two boys held their breath. Good gracious! They were right in the middle of something very queer! Why were these men meeting at this tumbledown place? Who were they and what were they doing? Where were Susie and Jeff, too? Were they listening and watching as well?

COME INTO THE NEXT ROOM. THERE ARE BOXES THERE TO SIT ON, AND A LIGHT WON'T SHINE OUT THERE AS MUCH AS IT DOES FROM THIS ROOM. COME ON, LARRY — HERE ZEB, SHINE YOUR TORCH IN FRONT.

Chapter 8
An uncomfortable time

THE two boys were half-glad, half-sorry that the men had gone into another room. Glad because they were now not afraid of being found, but sorry because it was now impossible to hear clearly what the men were saying.

They could hear a murmur from the next room.

Jack nudged George. 'I'm going to creep across the floor and go to the door. Perhaps I can hear what they are saying then,' he whispered.

'No, don't,' said George, in alarm. 'We'll be discovered. You're sure to make a noise!'

'I've got rubber-soled shoes on. I shan't make a sound,' whispered back Jack. 'You stay here, George. I DO wonder where Susie and Jeff are. I hope I don't bump into them anywhere.'

Jack made his way very quietly to the doorway that led to the next room. There was a broken door still hanging there, and he could peep through the

crack. He saw the three men in the room beyond, sitting on old boxes, intently studying a map of some kind, and talking in low voices.

If only he could hear what they said! He tried to see what the men were like, but it was too dark. He could only hear their voices, one an educated voice speaking clearly and firmly, and the other two rough and common.

Jack hadn't the slightest idea what they were talking about. Loading and unloading. Six-two or maybe seven-ten. Points, points, points. There mustn't be a moon. Darkness, fog, mist. Points. Fog. Six-two, but it might go as long as seven-twenty. And again, points, points, points.

What in the world could they be discussing? It was maddening to hear odd words like this that made no sense. Jack strained his ears to try and make out more, but it was no use, he couldn't. He decided to edge a little more nearer.

He leaned against something that gave way behind him. It was a cupboard door! Before he could stop himself Jack fell inside, landing with a soft thud. The door closed on him with a little click. He sat there, alarmed and astonished, not daring to move.

'What was that?' said one of the men.

They all listened, and at that moment a big rat ran silently round the room, keeping to the wall. One of the men picked it out in the light of his torch.

'Rats,' he said. 'This place is alive with them. That's what we heard.'

'I'm not sure,' said the man with the clear voice. 'Switch off that light, Zeb. Sit quietly for a bit and listen.'

The light was switched off. The men sat in utter silence, listening. Another rat scuttered over the floor.

Jack sat absolutely still in the cupboard, fearful that the men might come to find out who had made a noise. George stood in the hearth of the next room, wondering what had happened. There was such dead silence now, and darkness too!

The owl awoke in the chimney above him, and stirred once more. Night-time! It must go hunting! It gave one soft hoot and dropped down the chimney to make its way out through the bare window.

It was as startled to find George standing at the bottom of the chimney as George was startled to feel the owl brushing his cheek. It flew silently out of the window, a big moving shadow in the dimness.

George couldn't bear it. He must get out of this chimneyplace, he must! Something else might fall down on him and touch his face softly. Where was Jack? How mean of him to go off and leave him with things that lived in chimneys! And Jack had the torch with him too. George would have given anything to flick on the light of a torch.

He crept out of the hearth, and stood in the middle of the floor, wondering what to do. What *was* Jack doing? He had said he was going to the doorway that led to the next room, to see if he could hear what the men said. But were the men there now? There wasn't a sound to be heard.

Perhaps they have slipped out of another window and gone, thought poor George. If so why doesn't Jack come back? It's too bad of him. I can't bear this much longer.

He moved over to the doorway, putting out his hands to feel if Jack was

there. No, he wasn't. The next room was in black darkness, and he couldn't see a thing there. There was also complete silence. Where *was* everyone?

George felt his legs giving way at the knees. This horrible old tumbledown place! Why ever had he listened to Jack and come here with him? He was sure that Jeff and Susie hadn't been fatheads enough to come here at night.

He didn't dare to call out. Perhaps Jack was somewhere nearby, scared too. What about the Secret Seven password? What was it now? Cheeky Charlie!

If I whisper Cheeky Charlie, Jack will know it's me, he thought. It's our password. He'll know it's me, and he'll answer.

So he stood at the doorway and whispered: 'Cheeky Charlie! Cheeky Charlie!'

No answer. He tried again, a little louder this time, 'Cheeky Charlie!'

And then a torch snapped on, and caught him directly in its beam. A voice spoke to him harshly.

'What's all this? What do you know about Charlie? Come right into the room, boy, and answer my question.'

Night Hunters
of the Countryside

You may have read that rather spooky bit about the Secret Seven's adventure at Tigger's Barn when a quavering hoot comes to their ears. 'Maybe it's an owl,' George says at last. 'Yes, listen to it hooting.'

Well, not only owls hunt at night. Anyone who goes into the countryside after dark and sits very still should hear other rustlings and stirrings. Quite scary, really! It·is the time when many of our familiar animals come out to hunt. Some, being small, are quite surprising; others are more rarely seen.

The common shrew, a tiny mouse-like creature with a longish, pointed head, is a ferocious and quarrelsome bundle of fur. It is so delicate that a large raindrop falling near one has been known to cause death. Yet it fears little and can eat over three times its own weight in a day and dies unless it feeds every few hours. Its natural prey is worms, insects, and those of its own kind it has killed in fighting. Glands giving out a stong, unpleasant odour are its means of defence. Unfortunately, they are not enough to keep away owls and, in daylight, many other flesh-eaters.

Perhaps that is why shrews (and there are five different species in Britain) tend to be particularly active at night. The water shrew, a beautiful little creature, is a first-class swimmer, living on crus-taceans and water insects. In captivity it has been known to kill and eat frogs. Many country legends and superstitions about the shrew family abound.

Our common frog, able to live on land and in water, hunts by night and by day, preying chiefly on insects. Although varying in shades of colour, we have only one native species, this found almost everywhere. Our other two frogs, the marsh frog and the edible frog, were both introduced from abroad into this country. The marsh frog is quite a nuisance in some areas, croaking very loudly at night and preying on both newts and dragonflies. It destroys what many naturalists want to encourage.

The toad, another amphibian, hunts and travels mainly by night. Unlike the frog, it has a perfectly dry skin, one it always swallows upon shedding, which it does periodically. It lives entirely on slugs, worms and insects.

Bats, sometimes mistaken for birds, come out at dusk and hunt right through the night, feeding largely upon moths which, like all their food, they catch and eat on the wing. They also eat other small insects.

The greatest flying creature of

the night must be the silently pouncing owl, which is quite noiseless when it makes its deadly descent. Farmers greatly approve of it, for it is a destroyer of rodents and insects, though the little shrew might strongly object. The bar owl (or screech owl) is our most common, though several other species also breed here.

Because cats see so well in the dark it is obvious they will be excellent night hunters; not that most owners like them to stay out at night. The only true wild variety found in Britain, fortunately rare, is the Scottish Wildcat—now said to be increasing in the Highlands. It is savage, deadly and a very dangerous killer. Valuable game is often lost to it, and there is even a case on record of a man being killed. Although it resembles a rather large domestic 'tabby', it has nothing in common with friendly old 'puss'. Pound for pound, in fighting fury it is doubtful if any other creature can equal it.

The fox of course hunts at any time, night or day. By night he will now come into towns, forage in dustbins and often be the mysterious cause of many a domestic cat's disappearance. Few farmers will approve of the fox, though in appearance it can be strikingly handsome.

Much rarer, but also a hunter by night or by day, is the polecat, which is larger and more heavily built than the far commoner stoat. It is found in the Scottish Highlands and Wales, the Welsh polecat being very fierce indeed. It lives on game, rabbits, poultry, fish and eels, always hunting and killing more than it needs. Even man is known to have been attacked.

'Brock' the badger is very seldom seen anywhere except at night. With his black and white stripes along head and face, and his long snout, he is very easy to recognise. A cleanly, very attractive-looking creature, he even cleans his claws on a tree-trunk before entering 'home'. This is usually a deep burrow called a 'set', running many feet into the ground and often with more than one comfortable room. The badger is a great digger, his short, strong legs well suited to this.

Brock hunts and lives upon almost everything—wasps' nests, snakes, rabbits and slugs, also liking fruit and some roots. He is a sociable animal, often living in a warren of sets shared with other families. He is very shy of man—and with reason—although the cruel sport of badger-baiting has long been prohibited.

An amusing night hunter, one many of you have probably seen, is the hedgehog. His grunts and snores as he sleeps by day have been heard near many a back-garden compost heap. He is a surprisingly good swimmer and, usually seeming to be slow moving, can run quite quickly when he desires. He hunts and eats mice, slugs, worms, frogs, rats and snakes. He will catch an adder by first biting its tail and then tightly rolling himself up into a prickly ball. The infuriated adder kills itself by continually striking onto the needle-sharp spines. The hedgehog is a friendly little creature to have in the garden, and a saucer of bread-and-milk by your back door will be greatly appreciated. It is unwise to take him indoors, however, because Mum and Dad will not appreciate his fleas!

Another night hunter, often because he himself has been hunted, is the otter, a delightful, playful animal who seems to revel in fun. His lair, called a 'holt', is usually within the roots of a tree on a river bank, the main entry under water. There is generally a dry land entry or exit as well. Fish is his diet, and it takes a very smart one to outswim an otter!

Chapter 9
Very peculiar

GEORGE WAS ASTONISHED. WHY, THE MEN WERE STILL THERE! THEN WHERE WAS JACK? WHAT HAD HAPPENED TO HIM?

COME ON IN. WE HEARD YOU SAYING "CHEEKY CHARLIE". HAVE YOU GOT A MESSAGE FROM HIM?

A MESSAGE? FROM CHEEKY CHARLIE? WHY, THAT'S ONLY A PASSWORD. JUST THE NAME OF A DOG. WHAT DOES HE MEAN? WHAT IS GOING ON?

THEY CERTAINLY DID! AND MAYBE, THOUGHT GEORGE, IF HE PLAYED ALONG WITH THEM THEY WOULD DO THEIR BUSINESS AND LET HIM GO. BUT HOW WOULD HE KNOW WHAT TO SAY? THEN CAME A LUCKY BREAK...

WILL YOU COME INTO THE ROOM? WHAT'S THE MATTER WITH YOU, BOY? ARE YOU SCARED? WE SHAN'T EAT A MESSENGER FROM CHARLIE.

WAIT A MINUTE... COULD THERE BE SOMEONE CALLED CHARLIE, CHEEKY CHARLIE? AND DO THESE MEN THINK I'VE COME FROM HIM?

THE MAN WROTE IN A NOTE-BOOK, AND THEN...

TAKE THIS TO CHARLIE—AND DON'T GO CALLING HIM CHEEKY, SEE? SAUCY BOYS GET THEIR EARS BOXED.

NOW GEORGE HAD TO ANSWER, NOT EVEN KNOWING WHAT THE TWO NAMES MEANT...

DALLING'S!

OKAY. NOW CLEAR OFF. YOU'RE SCARED OF THIS PLACE, AREN'T YOU? WANT ME TO TAKE YOU DOWN THE HILL?

THERE WON'T BE NO MESSAGE FROM CHARLIE—HE'S WAITING FOR NEWS FROM US. I'LL SCRIBBLE A MESSAGE FOR HIM. CAN'T THINK WHY HE USES SUCH A DUMB KID, THOUGH.

WHERE'S CHARLIE NOW, KID? AT DALLING'S OR AT HAMMOND'S?

OUTSIDE, GEORGE WENT INTO HIDING, WAITING FOR THE MEN TO LEAVE SO THAT HE COULD FIND JACK. THEN, MINUTES LATER...

GOOD! I'LL JUST GIVE THEM A COUPLE OF MINUTES TO GET CLEAR.

THAT WAS THE LAST THING POOR GEORGE WANTED! HE TURNED QUICKLY AND MADE FOR THE WINDOW IN THE NEXT ROOM— ALL THE WHILE WONDERING WHAT HAD HAPPENED TO JACK...

BUT AS GEORGE ENTERED THE HOUSE AGAIN HE HAD ANOTHER SHOCK. FROM THE DOORWAY OF THE ROOM WHERE THE MEN HAD MET CAME A PIERCING WHISPER...

CHEEKY CHARLIE!

OH GOSH! IS THAT JACK... OR SOMEBODY ELSE WHO KNOWS CHARLIE?

BUT THEN...

IT IS YOU, GEORGE! WHY DIDN'T YOU ANSWER WHEN I SAID THE PASSWORD?

OH, JACK! WHERE WERE YOU? I'VE HAD A FRIGHTFUL TIME! WHERE HAVE YOU BEEN?

I FELL INTO THIS CUPBOARD AND IT SHUT ON ME. I COULDN'T HEAR A THING, AND I DIDN'T DARE MOVE IN CASE THOSE MEN CAME TO LOOK FOR ME.

OH, I SEE. SO YOU DIDN'T HEAR WHAT HAPPENED TO ME? THE MEN DISCOVERED ME, AND—

DISCOVERED YOU! WHAT DID THEY DO?

IT'S REALLY PECULIAR. I WHISPERED THE PASSWORD— "CHEEKY CHARLIE"— HOPING YOU WOULD HEAR IT, BUT THE MEN HEARD IT AND CALLED ME INTO THE ROOM— AND THEY ASKED ME IF I WAS A MESSENGER FROM HIM.

JACK DIDN'T FOLLOW THIS, SO GEORGE EXPLAINED THAT APPARENTLY THERE WAS A MAN NAMED CHEEKY CHARLIE, AND THAT THE THREE MEN THOUGHT HE WAS USING GEORGE AS A MESSENGER...

AND THEY GAVE ME A MESSAGE FOR HIM. IN A NOTE. I'VE GOT IT IN MY POCKET.

I SAY, THIS IS THRILLING. WE MIGHT BE IN THE MIDDLE OF AN ADVENTURE AGAIN. LET'S SEE THE NOTE.

NO, LET'S GO HOME AND THEN READ IT. I WANT TO GET OUT OF THIS OLD PLACE— I DON'T LIKE IT A BIT.

YES, BUT WAIT. WHAT ABOUT JEFF AND SUSIE? THEY MUST BE SOME-WHERE HERE TOO. WE OUGHT TO LOOK FOR THEM.

LET'S CALL THEM. THERE'S NOBODY ELSE HERE NOW. JEFF! SUSIE! COME ON OUT, WHEREVER YOU ARE!

43

GEORGE, I'M WORRIED. I KNOW SUSIE'S A NUISANCE, BUT SHE'S STILL MY SISTER. WE'D BETTER HURRY HOME AND TELL MOTHER THAT SHE'S DISAPPEARED, JEFF TOO. COME ON! SOMETHING MAY HAVE HAPPENED TO THEM!

THEY REACHED THE HOUSE JUST AS JACK'S MOTHER ARRIVED HOME...

MOTHER! SUSIE'S MISSING! SHE'S GONE! OH, MOTHER, SHE WENT TO TIGGER'S BARN, AND NOW SHE ISN'T THERE!

WHAT DO YOU MEAN? WHY DID SUSIE GO OUT!

BUT INSIDE...

HALLO, MOTHER! COME AND SEE JEFF'S RAILWAY GOING!

WHO CAME SPYING ON OUR FAMOUS FIVE MEETING, THEN? WHO HEARD ALL SORTS OF THINGS AND BELIEVED THEM? WHO'S BEEN TO TIGGER'S BARN IN THE DARK? WHO'S A SILLY-BILLY?

WHY, YOU —

JACK! STOP THAT AT ONCE! AND SUSIE, GO TO BED. JACK!

WHY, THERE'S SUSIE! WHATEVER DID YOU MEAN ABOUT HER DISAPPEARING JACK? WHAT A SILLY JOKE!

SHE'S A WICKED GIRL! SHE — SHE — SHE —

GO AND RUN YOUR BATH, JACK. YOU CAN BOTH GO WITHOUT YOUR SUPPER NOW. I WILL NOT HAVE THIS BEHAVIOUR.

JEFF QUICKLY GATHERED UP HIS RAILWAY THINGS, WITH GEORGE HELPING HIM. BOTH BOYS WERE SCARED OF JACK'S MOTHER WHEN SHE WAS CROSS, AND THEY DISAPPEARED OUT OF THE HOUSE AS QUICKLY AS THEY COULD...

...GEORGE EVEN FORGOT WHAT HE HAD IN HIS POCKET — A PENCILLED NOTE TO SOMEONE CALLED CHEEKY CHARLIE, WHICH HE HADN'T EVEN READ! WELL, WELL, WELL!

Chapter 10
Call a meeting!

GEORGE went quickly along the road with Jeff. Jeff chuckled.

'I say, you and Jack fell for our little trick beautifully, didn't you? Susie's clever, she laid her plan well. We all talked at the tops of our voices so that Jack would be sure to hear. We knew he was hiding in the laurel bush.'

George said nothing. He was angry that Susie and the Famous Five should have played a trick like that on the Secret Seven—angry that Jack had been so easily taken in— but, dear me, what curious results that trick had had!

Susie had mentioned Tigger's Barn just to make Jack and the Secret Seven think that the Famous Five had got hold of something that was going on there, and had talked about a make-believe Stumpy Dick and Twisty Tom. And lo and behold, something *was* going on there, not between Stumpy Dick and Twisty Tom, but between three mysteri-ous fellows called Zeb, Larry, and had he heard the other man's name? No, he hadn't.

'You're quiet, George,' said Jeff, chuckling again. 'How did you enjoy your visit to Tigger's Barn? I bet it was a bit frightening!'

'It was,' said George, truthfully, and said no more. He wanted to think about everything carefully, to sort out all he had heard, to try and piece together what had happened. It was all jumbled up in his mind.

One thing's certain, he thought, suddenly. We'll have to call a meeting of the Secret Seven. How queer that the Famous Five should have played a silly joke on us and led us to Something Big—another adventure, I'm sure. Susie's an idiot, but she's done the Secret Seven a jolly good turn!

As soon as George got home he felt in

his pocket for the note that Zeb had given him. He felt round anxiously. It would have been too dreadful if he had lost it!

But he hadn't. His fingers closed over the folded piece of paper. He took it out, his hand trembling with excitement.

Dear Charlie,
Everything's ready and going O.K. Can't see that anything can go wrong. but a fog would be very welcome as you can guess! Larry's looking after the points, we've arranged that. Don't forget the lorry, and get the tarpaulin truck cover marked with white at one corner. That'll save time in looking for the right load. It's clever of you to send out this load by truck and collect it by lorry! All the best Zeb.

George couldn't make head or tail of this. What in the world was it all about? There was a plot of some kind, that was clear, but what did everything else mean?

George went to the telephone. Perhaps Peter wouldn't yet be in bed. He really MUST get on to him and tell him something important had happened.

Peter was just going to bed. He came to the telephone in surprise, when his mother called him to it.

'Hallo! What's up?'

'Peter, I can't stop to tell you everything now, but we went to Tigger's Barn, Jack and I, and my word, there is something going on. We had quite an adventure, and—'

'You don't mean to tell me that that tale of Susie's was true!' said Peter, disbelievingly.

'No. At least, it was all made-up on her part, as you said, but all the same, something is going on at Tigger's Barn, Peter, something Susie didn't know about, of course, because she only mentioned the place in fun. But it's serious, Peter. You must call a meeting of the Secret Seven tomorrow evening after tea.'

There was a pause.

'Right,' said Peter, at last. 'I will. This is jolly queer, George. Don't tell me anything more over the phone, because I don't want Mother asking me too many questions. I'll tell Janet to tell Pam and Barbara there's a meeting tomorrow evening at five o'clock in our shed, and we'll tell Colin and Jack. Golly! This sounds pretty mysterious.'

'You just wait till you hear the whole story!' said George. 'You'll be amazed.'

He put down the receiver, and got ready for bed, quite forgetting that he had had no supper. He couldn't stop thinking about the happenings of the evening. How queer that the password of the Secret Seven should be Cheeky Charlie, and there should be a real fellow called by that name!

And how extraordinary that Susie's bit of make-believe should suddenly have come true without her knowing it! Something was going on at Tigger's Barn!

He got into bed and lay awake for a long time. Jack was also lying awake thinking. He was excited. He wished he hadn't been shut up in that silly cupboard, when he might have been listening all the time. Still, George seemed to have got quite a lot of information.

The Secret Seven were very thrilled the next day. It was difficult not to let the Famous Five see that they had something exciting on hand, but Peter had strictly forbidden anyone to talk about the matter at school, just in *case* that tiresome Susie, with her long ears, got to hear of it.

'We don't want the Famous Five trailing us around,' said Peter. 'Just wait till this evening, all of you, and then we'll really get going!'

At five o'clock every single member of the Secret Seven was in the shed in Peter's garden. All of them had raced home quickly after afternoon school, gobbled their teas, and come rushing to the meeting.

The password was whispered quickly, as one after another passed into the shed, each wearing the badge with S.S. on. 'Cheeky Charlie, Cheeky Charlie, Cheeky Charlie.'

Jack and George had had little time to exchange more than a few words with one another. They were bursting to tell their strange story!

'Now, we're all here,' said Peter. 'Scamper, sit by the door and keep guard. Bark if you hear anything at all. This is a most important meeting.'

Scamper got up and went solemnly to the door. He sat down by it, listening, looking very serious.

'Oh, do buck up, Peter,' said Pam. 'I can't wait a minute more to hear what it's all about!'

'All right, all right,' said Peter. 'You know that we weren't going to call another meeting till the Christmas hols, unless something urgent happened. Well, it's happened. Jack, you start off with the story, please.'

Jack was only too ready to tell it. He described how he had hidden in the laurel bush to overhear what the Famous Five said at their meeting in the summer-house. He repeated the ridiculous make-up that Susie had invented to deceive the Secret Seven, and to send them off on a wild-goose chase just to make fun of them.

He told them how Peter had laughed at the story and said it *was* a make-up of Susie's, but how he and George had decided to go to Tigger's Barn just in case it wasn't.

'But I was right,' interrupted Peter. 'It *was* a make-up, but just by chance there was some truth in it, too, though Susie didn't know.'

George took up the tale. He told the others how he and Jack had gone to Tigger's Barn, thinking that Susie and Jeff were in front of them. And then came the thrilling part of their adventure in the old tumbledown house!

Everyone listened intently, the girls holding their breath when George came to the bit where the three men arrived.

Then Jack told how he went to the doorway to listen, and fell into the cupboard, and George told how he had gone to look for Jack, and had said the password, Cheeky Charlie, which had had such surprising results.

'Do you mean to say, there actually *is* a man called Cheeky Charlie?' asked Barbara, in amazement. 'Our password is only the name of a dog. Just fancy there being a *man* called that, too! My goodness!'

'Don't interrupt,' said Peter. 'Go on, both of you.'

Everyone sat up with wide eyes when George told how the men had thought he was a messenger from Cheeky Charlie, and when he told them about the note they had given him, and produced it from his pocket, the Secret Seven were speechless with excitement!

The note was passed from hand to hand. Peter rapped on a box at last.

'We've all seen the note now,' he said. 'And we've heard Jack and George tell what happened last night. It's quite clear that we've hit on something queer again. Do the Secret Seven think we should try and solve this new mystery?'

Everyone yelled and rapped on boxes, and Scamper barked in excitement too.

'Right,' said Peter. 'I agree too. But we have got to be very, very careful this time, or else the Famous Five will try and interfere, and they might spoil everything.

NOBODY—must say a single word about this to anyone in the world. Is that agreed?'

It was. Scamper came up and laid a big paw on Peter's knee, as if he thoroughly agreed too.

'Go back to the door, Scamper,' said Peter. 'We depend on you to give us warning if any of those tiresome Famous Five come snooping round. On guard, Scamper.'

Scamper trotted back to his place by the door obediently. The Seven crowded more closely together, and began a grand discussion.

'First, let's sort out all the things that Jack and George heard,' said Peter. 'Then we'll try and make out what they mean. At the moment I'm in a muddle about everything and haven't the slightest idea what the men are going to do.'

'Right,' said Jack. 'Well, as I told you, I heard the men talking, but their voices were very low, and I could only catch words now and again.'

'What words were they?' asked Peter. 'Tell us carefully.'

'Well, they kept saying something about "loading and unloading",' said Jack. 'And they kept on and on mentioning "points".'

'What sort of points?' asked Peter.

Jack shook his head, completely at a loss.

'I've no idea. They mentioned figures too. They said "six-two" quite a lot of times, and then they said "maybe seventen". And they said there mustn't be a moon, and I heard them talk about darkness, fog, and mist. Honestly, I couldn't make head or tail of it. I only know they must have been discussing some plan.'

'What else did you hear?' asked Janet.

'Nothing,' answered Jack. 'I fell into the cupboard then, and when the door shut on me I couldn't hear another word.'

'And all *I* can add is that the men asked me if Cheeky Charlie was at Dalling's or Hammond's,' said George. 'But goodness knows what *that* meant.'

'Perhaps they are the name of a workshop or works of some kind,' suggested Colin. 'We could find out.'

'Yes. We might be able to trace those,' said Peter. 'Now, this note. Whatever can it mean? It's got the word "points" here again. And they talk about trucks and lorries. It's plain that there's some robbery planned, I think. But what kind? They want fog, too. Well, that's understandable, I suppose.'

'Shall we take the note to the police?' said Barbara, suddenly gripped by a bright idea.

'Oh no! Not yet!' said George. 'It's *my* note and I'd like to see if we can't do something about it ourselves before we tell any grown-ups. After all, we've managed lots of affairs very well so far. I don't see why we shouldn't be able to do something about this one too.'

'I'm all for trying,' said Peter. 'It's jolly exciting. And we've got quite a lot to go on, really. We know the names of three of the four men—Zeb, which is probably short for Zebedee, a most unusual name; and Larry, probably short for Laurence; and Cheeky Charlie, who is perhaps the boss.'

'Yes, and we know he's at Dalling's or Hammond's,' said Jack. 'What do we do first, Peter?'

Scamper suddenly began to bark wildly and scrape at the door.

'Not another word!' said Peter, sharply. 'There's someone outside!'

Strange Coincidences

It was very odd how Susie made up a story about Tigger's Barn, to fool the Secret Seven, which turned out to be true! But there are quite a few strange coincidences to be found in history, if you look carefully enough.

Perhaps one of the most startling coincidences on record occurred during World War I when a young fighter pilot flying in a single cockpit machine (they were not strapped in) started a loop. The aircraft was at the top of the loop, upside down, when he fell out and plummeted earthwards. Incredible as it may seem, the aircraft completed its loop under power and he fell back into his own cockpit, to actually regain control. The odds against this lucky coincidence must be tremendous.

When the famous tomb of the Egyptian boy king Tutankhamun was opened in 1923 at Luxor where he had lain undisturbed for some 3,000 years, a warning was found — 'Death will come to those who disturb the sleep of the Pharaohs.' Within a few weeks of

breaking into the tomb, the expedition's leader Lord Carnarvon was dead, apparently from an infected mosquito bite. Premature death had within six years claimed twelve others who had been present when the Luxor tomb was opened.

In 1970, when the sole survivor of the expedition, Richard Adamson, then aged 70, appeared on television to 'explode the myth' of the death curse, he was on his way home when his taxi collided with a tractor and he had a very narrow escape. All in all, a series of startling coincidences.

On the morning of October 5, 1930, Britain's ill-fated airship the R 101 crashed onto a wooded hillside in France and exploded into flames, only six of the fifty-odd people aboard miraculously escaping. Strangely enough, one young engineer had refused to make the flight, having a dread premonition that disaster would overtake the airship. He watched the great ship take off from Cardington and then set out home on his motorcycle — to crash headlong into a lorry and be instantly killed.

Unlucky coincidences always tend to be more faithfully recorded than lucky ones, probably because bad news is more dramatic than good. However, there are many, many instances in which some strange freak of chance has prevented a person from making a journey which, for others, ended very unfortunately.

Probably you know of some strange personal coincidence yourself; nearly everybody can think of at least one!

Chapter II
Any ideas?

Peter opened the door. Scamper tore out, barking. Then he stopped by a bush and wagged his tail. The Secret Seven ran to him.

A pair of feet showed at the bottom of the bush. Jack gave a shout of rage and pushed into the bush. He dragged someone out—Susie!

'How dare you!' he yelled. 'Coming here and listening! How dare you, Susie?'

'Let me go,' said Susie. 'I like you asking me how I dare! I'm only copying what *you* did on Saturday! Who hid in the laurel bush, and—'

'How did you know we were having a meeting?' demanded Jack, shaking Susie.

'I just followed you,' said Susie, grinning. 'But I didn't hear anything because I didn't dare to go near the door,

in case Scamper barked. I did a sudden sneeze, though, and he must have heard me. What are you calling a meeting about?'

'As if we'd tell you!' said Peter, crossly. 'Go on home, Susie. Go on! Jack, take her home. The meeting is over.'

'Blow!' said Jack. 'All right. Come on, Susie. And if I have any nonsense from you, I'll pull your hair till you yell!'

Jack went off with Susie. Peter faced round to the others and spoke in a low voice.

'Listen. All of you think hard about what has been said, and give me or Janet any good ideas tomorrow. It's no good going on with this meeting. Somebody else belonging to the Famous Five might come snooping round too.'

'Right,' said the Secret Seven, and

went home, excited and very much puzzled. *How* could they think of anything that would help to piece together the jumble of words they knew? Points. Six-two, seven-ten. Fog, mist, darkness. Dalling's. Hammond's.

Each of them tried to think of some good idea. Barbara could think of nothing at all. Pam tried asking her father about Dalling's or Hammond's. He didn't know either of them. Pam felt awkward when he asked her why she wanted to know, and didn't go on with the subject.

Colin decided that a robbery was going to be done one dark and foggy night, and that the goods were to be unloaded from a lorry somewhere. He couldn't imagine why they were to be sent in a truck. All the boys thought exactly the same thing, but, as Peter said, it wasn't much help because they didn't know what date, what place, or what lorry!

Then Jack had quite a good idea. He thought it would be helpful if they tried to find a man called Zebedee, because surely he must be the Zeb at Tigger's Barn. There couldn't be *many* Zebedees in the district!

'All right, Jack. It's a good *idea*,' said Peter. 'You can do the finding out for us. Produce this Zeb, and that may be the first step.'

'Yes, but how shall I find out?' said Jack. 'I can't go round asking every man I meet if he's called Zeb.'

'No. That's why I said it was a good *idea*,' said Peter, grinning. 'But that's about all it is. It's an impossible thing to do, you see; so that's why it will remain just a good idea and nothing else. Finding the only Zebedee in the district would be like looking for a needle in a haystack.'

'I shouldn't like to have to do *that*,' said Janet, who was with them. 'Peter and I have got about the only good idea, I think, Jack.'

'What's that?' asked Jack.

'Well, we looked in our telephone directory at home to see if any firm called Dalling or Hammond was there,' said Janet. 'But there wasn't, so we thought they must be somewhere farther off, not in our district at all. Our telephone book only gives the names of people in this area, you see.'

'And now we're going to the post-office to look in the big telephone directories there,' said Peter. 'They give the names of districts much farther away. Like to come with us?'

Jack went with them. They came to the post-office and went in. Peter took up two telephone books, one with the D's in and one with the H's.

'Now I'll look for Dalling,' he said, and thumbed through the D's. The other two leaned over him, looking down the D's too.

'Dale, Dale, Dale, Dales, Dalgleish, Daling, Dalish, Dallas, DALLING!' read Peter, his finger following down the list of names. 'Here it is—Dalling. Oh, there are three Dallings! Blow!'

'There's a Mrs A. Dalling, Rose Cottage, Hubley,' said Janet. 'And E. A. Dalling, of Manor House, Tallington, and Messrs. E. Dalling, Manufacturers of Lead Goods. Well—which would be the right Dalling? The manufacturers, I suppose.'

'Yes,' said Peter, sounding excited. 'Now for the H's. Where are they? In the other book. Here we are—Hall, Hall— goodness, what a lot of people are called Hall! Hallet, Ham, Hamm, Hammers, Hamming, Hammond, Hammond, Hammond, Hammond— oh, LOOK!'

They all looked. Peter was pointing to the fourth name of Hammond. 'Hammond and Co. Ltd. Lead manufacturers. Petlington.'

'There you are,' said Peter, triumphantly. 'Two firms dealing in lead, one called Hammond, one called Dalling. Cheeky Charlie must be something to do with both.'

'Lead!' said Jack. 'It's very valuable nowadays, isn't it? I'm always reading about thieves going and stealing it off church roofs. I don't know why churches so often have lead roofs, but they seem to.'

'It looks as if Cheeky Charlie might be going to send a load of lead off somewhere in a truck, and Zeb and the others are going to stop it, and take the lead,' said Peter. 'As you say, it's very valuable, Jack.'

'Charlie must have quite a high position if he's in both firms,' said Janet. 'Oh dear—I do wonder what his real name is! Cheeky Charlie! I wonder why

they call him that?'

'Because he's bold and has got plenty of cheek, I expect,' said Peter. 'If only Hammond's and Dalling's weren't so far away! We could go and snoop round there and see if we could hear of anyone called Cheeky Charlie.'

'They're miles away,' said Jack, looking at the addresses. 'Well, we've been quite clever, but I don't see that we've got very much farther, really. We just know that Dalling's and Hammond's are firms that deal in lead, which is very valuable stuff, but that's all!'

'Yes. It doesn't take us very far,' said Peter, shutting up the directory. 'We'll have to think a bit harder. Come on, let's go and buy some sweets. Sucking a bit of toffee always seems to help my thinking!'

Chapter 12

A game - and a brain-wave!

ANOTHER day went by, and Saturday came. A meeting was called for that morning, but nobody had much to say. In fact, it was rather a dull meeting after the excitement of the last one. The Seven sat in the shed eating biscuits provided by Jack's mother, and Scamper was at the door, on guard as usual.

It was raining outside. The Seven looked out dismally.

'No good going for a walk, or having a game of football,' said Peter. 'Let's stay here in the shed and play a game.'

'Fetch your railway set, Peter,' said Janet. 'And I'll fetch the farm set. We could set out the lines here in the midst of the toy trees and farm buildings, looking as if they were real countryside. We've got simply heaps of farm stuff.'

'Oh yes. Let's do that,' said Pam. 'I love your farm set. It's the nicest and biggest I've ever seen. Do get it! We girls could set it out, and the boys could put up the railway.'

'It's a jolly good thing to do on a rainy morning like this,' said Jack, pleased. 'I wanted to help Jeff with *his* fine railway the other day, when George came to tea with me, but he was Susie's guest, and she wouldn't have let us join in for anything. You know, she's very suspicious that we're working on something, Peter. She keeps on and on at me to tell her if anything happened at Tigger's Barn that night.'

'Well, just shut her up,' said Peter. 'Scamper, you needn't watch the door any more. You can come and join us, old fellow. The meeting's over.'

Scamper was pleased. He ran round everyone, wagging his tail. Peter fetched his railway set, and Janet and Pam went to get the big farm set. It had absolutely everything, from animals and farm men to trees, fences, troughs and sties!

They all began to put up the two sets—the boys putting together the lines, and girls setting out a proper little countryside, with trees, fences, animals and farm buildings. It really was fun.

Peter suddenly looked up at the window. He had noticed a movement there. He saw a face looking in, and leapt up with such a fierce yell that everyone jumped in alarm.

'It's Jeff,' he cried. 'I wonder if he's snooping round for the Famous Five? After him, Scamper!'

But Jeff had taken to his heels, and, even if Scamper had caught him, nothing would have happened, because the spaniel knew Jeff well and liked him.

'It doesn't really matter Jeff looking in,' said Janet. 'All he'd see would be us having a very peaceful game! Let him stand out in the rain and look in if he wants to!'

The railway lines were ready at last. The three beautiful clockwork engines were attached to their line of trucks. Two were passenger trains and one was a goods train.

'I'll manage one train, you can do another train, Colin, and you can have a third one, Jack,' said Peter. 'Janet, you do the signals. You're good at those. And, George, you work the points. We mustn't have an accident. You can always switch one of the trains on to another line, if two look like crashing.'

'Right. I'll manage the points,' said George, pleased. 'I like doing those. I

love seeing a train being switched off a main-line into a siding.'

The engines were wound up and set going. They tore round the floor, and George switched them cleverly from one line to another when it seemed there might be an accident.

And, in the middle of all this, Janet suddenly sat up straight, and said in a loud voice: 'WELL, I NEVER!'

The others looked at her.

'What's the matter?' said Peter. 'Well, I never *what*? Why are you looking as if you are going to burst?'

'Points!' said Janet, excitedly. 'Points!' And she waved her hand to where George was sitting working the points, switching the trains from one line to another. 'Oh Peter, don't be so *stupid*! Don't you remember? Those men at Tigger's Barn talked about *points*. Jack said they kept *on* mentioning them. Well, I bet they were *points on some railway line*!'

There was a short silence. Then everyone spoke at once. 'Yes! It could be! Why didn't we think of it before? Of course! Points on the railway!'

The game stopped at once and an eager discussion began.

'Why should they use the points? It must be because they want to switch a train on to another line.'

'Yes, a train that contains something they want to steal—lead, probably!'

'Then it's a goods train. One of the trucks must be carrying the lead they want to steal!'

'The tarpaulin! Would that be covering up the load? Don't you remember? It had to be marked with white at the corner, so that the men would know it.'

'Yes! They wouldn't have to waste time then looking into every truck to see which was the right one. Sometimes there are thirty or forty trucks on a goods train. The white marks on the tarpaulin would tell them at once they had the right truck!'

'Woof,' said Scamper, joining in the general excitement.

Peter turned to him. 'Hey, Scamper, on guard at the door again, old fellow!' he said, at once. 'The meeting's begun again! On guard!'

Scamper went on guard. The Secret Seven drew close together, suddenly very excited. To think that one simple word had set their brains working like this, and put them on the right track at once!

'You are really clever, Janet,' said Jack, and Janet beamed.

'Oh, anyone might have thought of it,' she said. 'It just rang a bell in my mind somehow, when you kept saying "points". Oh, Peter, where are these points, do you think?'

Peter was following out another idea in his mind. 'I've thought of something else,' he said, his eyes shining. 'Those figures the men kept saying. Six-two, seven-ten. Couldn't they be the times of trains?'

'Oh *yes*! Like when we say Daddy's going to catch the six-twenty home, or the seven-twelve!' cried Pam. 'Six-two—there must be a train that starts somewhere at six-two. Or arrives somewhere then.'

'And they want a foggy or misty, dark night, because then it would be easy to switch the train into some siding,' said

56

Jack. 'A foggy night would be marvellous for them. The engine-driver couldn't possibly see that his train had been switched off on the wrong line. He'd go on till he came to some signal, and the men would be there ready to take the lead from the marked truck—'

'And they'd deal with the surprised engine-driver, and the guard too, I suppose,' said Colin.

There was a silence after this. It suddenly dawned on the Seven that there must be quite a big gang engaged in this particular robbery.

'I think we ought to tell somebody,' said Pam.

Peter shook his head. 'No. Let's find out more if we can. And I'm sure we can now! For instance, let's get a time-table and see if there's a train that arrives anywhere at two minutes past six—6.2.'

'That's no good,' said Jack, at once. 'Goods trains aren't in the time-tables.'

'Oh no. I forgot that,' said Peter. 'Well, what about one or two of us boys going down to the station and asking a few questions about goods trains and what time they come in, and where from? We know where the firms of Dalling and Hammond are. Where was it now—Petlington, wasn't it?'

'Yes,' said Janet. 'That's a good idea of yours to go down to the station, Peter. It's stopped raining. Why don't you go now?'

'I will,' said Peter. 'You come with me, Colin. Jack and George have had plenty of excitement so far, but you haven't had very much. Come on down to the station with me.'

So off went the two boys, looking rather thrilled. They really were on the trail now!

Peter and Colin arrived at the station

just as a train was coming in. They watched it. Two porters were on the platform, and a man stood with them in dirty blue overalls. He had been working on the line, and had hopped up on to the platform when the train came rumbling in.

The boys waited till the train had gone out. Then they went up to one of the porters.

'Are there any goods trains coming through?' asked Peter. 'We like watching them.'

'There's one in fifteen minutes' time,' said the porter.

'Is it a very long one?' asked Colin. 'I once counted forty-seven trucks pulled by a goods engine.'

'The longest one comes in here in the evening,' said the porter. 'How many trucks do you reckon it has as a rule, Zeb?'

The man in dirty overalls rubbed a black hand over his face, and pushed back his cap. 'Well, maybe thirty, maybe forty. It depends.'

The boys looked at one another. *Zeb!* The porter had called the linesman *Zeb!* Could it be—could it *possibly* be the same Zeb that had met the other two men at Tigger's Barn?

They looked at him. He wasn't much to look at, certainly, a thin, mean-faced little man, very dirty, and with hair much too long. Zeb! It was such an unusual name that the boys felt sure they must be face to face with the Zeb who had been up at the old tumbledown house.

'Er—what time does this goods train come in the evening?' asked Peter, finding his tongue at last.

'It comes in about six o'clock twice a week,' said Zeb. 'Six-two, it's supposed to be here, but sometimes it's late.'

'Where does it come from?' asked Colin.

'Plenty of places!' said Zeb. 'Turleigh, Idlesston, Hayley, Garton, Petlington. . . .'

'Petlington!' said Colin, before he could stop himself. That was the place where the firms of Dalling and Hammond were. Peter scowled at him, and Colin hurried to cover up his mistake in calling attention to the town they were so interested in.

'Petlington, yes, go on, where else?' said Colin.

The linesman gave him another string of names, and the boys listened. But they had learnt already a good deal of what they wanted to know.

The 6.2 was a goods train, that came in twice a week, and Petlington was one of the places it came from, probably with a truck or two added there, full of lead goods from Hammond's and Dalling's! Lead pipes? Sheets of lead? The boys had no idea, and it didn't really matter. It was lead, anyway, valuable lead, they were sure of that! Lead sent off by Cheeky Charlie for his firms.

'We've been playing with my model railway this morning,' said Peter, suddenly thinking of a way to ask about points and switches. 'It's a fine one, it's got points to switch my trains from one line to another. Jolly good they are too, as good as real points!'

'Ah, you want to ask my mate about *them*,' said Zeb. 'He's got plenty to deal with. He uses them to switch the goods trains from one part of the line to another. They often have to go into sidings, you know.'

'Does he switch the 6.2 into a siding?' said Peter. 'Or does it go straight through on the main-line?'

'Straight through,' said Zeb. 'No, Larry only switches the goods trains that have to be unloaded near here. The 6.2 goes right on to Swindon. You'll see it this evening if you come down.'

Peter had given a quick look at Colin to see if he had noticed the name of Zeb's mate—Larry! Zeb and Larry—what an enormous piece of luck! Colin gave a quick wink at Peter. Yes, he had noticed all right! He began to look excited.

'I wish we could see Larry working the points,' said Peter. 'It must be fun. I

expect the switches are quite different from the ones on my railway lines at home.'

Zeb laughed. 'You bet they are! Ours take some moving! Look, would you like to walk along the line with me, and I'll show you some switches that send a train off into a siding? It's about a mile up the line.'

Peter took a look at his watch. He would be very late for his dinner, but this was really important. Why, he might see the very points that Larry was going to use one dark, foggy night!

'Look out the kids don't get knocked down by a train,' the porter warned Zeb, as the linesman took the two boys down on to the track with him.

The boys looked at him with scorn. As if they couldn't tell when a train was coming!

It seemed a very long way up the line. Zeb had a job of work not far from the points. He left his tools by the side of the line he was to repair, and took the boys to where a number of lines crossed one another. He explained how the points worked.

'You pull this lever for that line, see? Watch how the rails move so that they lead to that other line over there, instead of letting the train keep on this line.'

Colin and Peter did a little pulling of levers themselves, and they found it

exceptionally hard work.

'Does the 6.2 come on this line?' asked Peter, innocently.

'Yes. But it goes straight on; it doesn't get switched to one side,' said Zeb. 'It never has goods for this district; it goes on to Swindon. Now don't you ever mess about on the railway by yourselves, or the police will be after you straight away!'

'We won't,' promised the two boys.

'Well, I must get on with my job,' said Zeb, not sounding as if he wanted to at all. 'So long! Hope I've told you what you wanted to know.'

He certainly had, much, much more than he imagined. Colin and Peter could hardly believe their luck. They made their way to the side of the line, and stood there for a while.

'We ought really to go and explore the siding,' said Peter. 'But we're so frightfully late. Blow! We forgot to ask what evenings the goods train comes in from Petlington!'

'Let's get back, and come again this afternoon,' said Colin. 'I'm frightfully hungry. We can find out the two days the goods train comes through when we're here this afternoon, and explore the siding too.'

They left the railway and went to the road. They were so excited that they could hardly stop talking. 'Fancy bumping into Zeb! Zeb himself! And hearing about Larry in charge of the points! Why, everything's as plain as can be. What a good thing Janet had the brain-wave this morning about points! My goodness, we're in luck's way!'

'We'll be back this afternoon as soon as we can,' said Peter. 'I vote the whole lot of us go. My word, this *is* getting exciting!'

TRAINS

With the coming of the diesel-electric and then fully electric trains much of the romance has gone out of train-watching and railways in general. There was something about the steam locomotive, its power and its sound, that caught the imagination of people everywhere. The variety of engines, the glowing firebox, the billowing smoke and steam were the stuff dreams are made of. One cannot imagine a famous book like 'The Ghost Train' being written around an electric one! Still, the romance of the past still remains.

It all started after the Scottish engineer, James Watt, had built his famous rotating shaft steam engine. This excited a great number of experimenters and led to Richard Trevithick building a steam-carriage suitable for use on road and on rail, the first to ever draw passengers. In Wales, 1804, his first practical rail locomotive was put into use.

The next development came from the two famous Stephensons, father and son, who despite all opposition and odds succeeded in building the now legendary 'Rocket'. It won the famous Rainhill locomotive race against three others, reaching the then almost impossible speed of thirty-five miles per hour. In fact, one of the judges still refused to believe that any vehicle could move faster than

ten. He must have been very upset!

This sensational race, for which thousands turned up to cheer, made the Rocket and its inventors celebrities. On September 15, 1830, the Liverpool and Manchester Railway opened in triumph in the presence of the great Duke of Wellington. The Age of the Train had really dawned!

With it came the greatest construction programme ever known at that time. Gangs of 'navvies'—formerly the 'navigators' who had dug Britain's canals—turned their attention to the construction

of railways. They were violent, savage men who largely terrorised surrounding neighbourhoods, but their work rate was incredible.

So trains and the railways had come to stay; the trouble was they

needed the support and approval of the influential upper classes. They were regarded as uncomfortable, dangerous and only suitable for commerce or the 'lower' classes. The rich and powerful continued to travel in their own private horse-coaches; only their servants would make the journey by train.

The Railway Act of 1844 demanded that Third Class railway coaches should be weatherproof; or rather that one such coach should be provided each day. Most were just open wagons, but the Act insisted on the provision of plank seats, lighting to be provided by means of open shutters near the roof. In bad weather the luckless passengers sat in stuffy near-darkness.

It was not until Queen Victoria, using the Great Western Railway, travelled in a gorgeous, specially built Royal Carriage from Slough to Paddington—her first ever rail journey—that opinions changed. She was delighted, and cheering crowds uproariously approved. From that moment the Age of the Train became Respectable!

Once popularly established, the other problems around trains and railways were not slow to emerge. The companies, all famous names, were privately owned and in bitter rivalry with each other. To further complicate matters there was no standard gauge for the rails; three different ones actually existed. It is easy to imagine the confusion this caused when broad and narrow-gauge lines had to meet at some point. Annoyed passengers had to change trains and expensive goods were delayed or often damaged in the changeover.

It was too late for Parliament to pass a law that would insist on one standard gauge for the whole country. The times were troubled already and the needed 'ruthless' action was more than any Govern-

ment dare risk. Things only really sorted themselves out when the Great Western Railway decided in its own interest to conform to the generally used 4ft. 8½in. gauge. It was expensive, for many of their tracks had to be altered.

Since speeds had increased with the traffic, safety began to be very important. The marvellous and complex safety systems of today were only in their infancy then. Bad accidents happened; sometimes

even an engine boiler blew up. Engineers and experts worked ceaselessly to overcome the weaknesses which kept coming to light.

All locomotive men dreamed of producing a real 'driver's engine', and the excellence of their work

soon showed itself. The good but earlier 'Drummond' locomotives, which tended to run out of steam, were replaced by 'Dunalastairs', an excellent design originating from Scotland and greatly influened by a locomotive inspector named McIntosh. It was a big boiler loco' capable of pulling some 150 tons, and amazingly fast. The Great Northern Railway even managed to improve on its size, a sensation in 1902.

With all the new glamour and speed came the dining-cars, buffet-cars and sleeping-cars; there were Railway Guides, Excursion Trains and Boat Trains. Tunnels were bored, bridges built and a vast network linked everywhere to somewhere else. But by September 27, 1935, a very significant event occurred—Britain's first fully streamlined high-speed train, the 'Silver Jubilee', set up a new rail-speed record, averaging above 100 miles per hour over some twenty-five miles.

The reason for this event was the increasing challenge to steam, particularly on the Continent, of the new diesel and diesel-electric engines. Britain, always happy with and confident of steam, felt the challenge had to be met.

Sadly it really signalled the steam locomotive's battle for survival, a battle started by financial and economic considerations and a greater need of general simplicity. Soon gone for ever were the famous 'Cornish Riviera Express' and the 'Mid-day Scot'. It was a battle the steam locomotive was fated to lose.

Chapter 13
An exciting afternoon

AFTER LUNCH THE SEVEN WERE CALLED TOGETHER, AND PETER TOLD THEM HOW HE AND COLIN HAD MET ZEB, AND HOW HE HAD TOLD THEM SO MUCH OF WHAT THEY WANTED TO KNOW...

HE DIDN'T REALISE WHY WE ASKED HIM SO MANY QUESTIONS. I MUST SAY HE WAS NICE TO US, THOUGH HE'S A MEAN LOOKING FELLOW!

WE'LL GO TO THE SIDING AND FIND OUT WHAT DAYS THAT GOODS TRAIN COMES ALONG!

SO THEY WENT TO THE STATION, AND PETER GOT TALKING TO THE PORTER...

HERE COMES ONE. IT WON'T STOP AT THE STATION, THOUGH — NO PASSENGERS TO GET ON OR OFF. WANT TO COUNT THE TRUCKS?

I'D LIKE TO SEE THAT GOODS TRAIN ZEB TOLD US ABOUT. THE ONE THAT COMES FROM PETLINGTON — THE 6.2, I THINK HE SAID.

YOU'D HAVE TO COME ON TUESDAY OR FRIDAY. BUT ITS DARK THEN!

IT'S A WONDER THINGS AREN'T STOLEN OUT OF THOSE OPEN TRUCKS!

OH, THEY ARE. THERE'S BEEN A LOT OF STEALING LATELY. SOME GANG AT WORK, THEY SAY.

WELL, I MUST GO AND DO A SPOT OF WORK. SO LONG, KIDS!

AFTER THEY'D WALKED FOR ABOUT A MILE...

THAT'S WHERE THEY PLAN TO SWITCH THE GOODS TRAIN OFF TO A SIDE-LINE. I WISH WE KNEW WHICH EVENING.

I THINK IT MUST BE SOON BECAUSE THAT NOTE THE MEN GAVE ME SAID THAT EVERYTHING WAS READY AND GOING OK.

THEY DECIDED TO FOLLOW THE SIDE-LINE...

THIS IS A LONELY PLACE. IF A GOODS TRAIN WAS DIVERTED DOWN HERE, NOBODY WOULD HEAR IT OR SEE IT.

I BET THERE WILL BE A LORRY CREEPING IN HERE SOME EVENING, READY TO TAKE THE LEAD SHEETS OR PIPES OR WHATEVER THEY ARE.

WHAT ABOUT COMING HERE ON TUESDAY EVENING, JUST IN CASE THAT'S THE NIGHT THEY'VE ARRANGED?

ONLY US BOYS. THEN BEFORE ZEB AND LARRY AND THE OTHERS COULD FINISH THEIR UNLOADING WE COULD GET THE POLICE HERE.

PERHAPS WE OUGHT TO CONTACT THAT BIG INSPECTOR WE LIKE. WE KNOW QUITE ENOUGH NOW.

YES. THE ONLY THING WE DON'T KNOW IS WHETHER IT'S THIS TUESDAY OR NOT!

I'D LIKE TO SEE THOSE POINTS. SHOW ME THEM, PETER. WE'LL LOOK OUT FOR TRAINS!

PETER FORGOT THAT CHILDREN WERE NOT ALLOWED TO TRESPASS ON THE RAILWAY LINES...

HEY, WHAT DO YOU THINK YOU'RE DOING? YOU COME BACK HERE.

LET'S RUN! DON'T LET HIM CATCH US.

NO. WE CAN'T RUN. I FORGOT WE OUGHT NOT TO WALK ON THE LINES LIKE THIS. COME BACK AND EXPLAIN.

THERE'S BEEN TOO MUCH TROUBLE FROM CHILDREN ON THE RAILWAYS LATELY. I'VE A GOOD MIND TO TELL YOUR PARENTS!

BUT WE WEREN'T DOING A THING, HONESTLY.

WHAT ARE YOU DOING IN THIS HERE GOODS YARD? UP TO SOME MISCHIEF?

WE'RE NOT!

WELL, WHAT **DID** YOU COME HERE FOR? YOU DIDN'T COME HERE FOR NOTHING.

TELL HIM!

OHO! SO THERE WAS SOMETHING YOU WERE AFTER! NOW YOU JUST TELL ME, OR I'LL TAKE YOUR NAMES AND ADDRESSES.

Peter wasn't going to tell this bad-tempered fellow anything. For one thing, he wouldn't believe the extraordinary tale that the Secret Seven had to tell, and for another, Peter wasn't going to give all his secrets away! It ended in the big policeman taking down all their names and addresses — and to think they had come there to help catch a gang of clever thieves!

I'LL GET TOLD OFF IF MY FATHER HEARS ABOUT THIS, LET'S TELL OUR NICE INSPECTOR EVERYTHING BEFORE THAT POLICEMAN GOES ROUND TO OUR PARENTS.

NO! WE'LL SETTLE THIS OURSELVES, AND THE POLICE CAN COME IN AT THE LAST MOMENT.

I'D LIKE TO COME, TOO, ON THAT NIGHT.

WELL, YOU WON'T. NO GIRLS AT ALL.

LOOK AT BARBARA, CRYING OVER A POLICEMAN TAKING HER NAME AND ADDRESS! WHAT USE WOULD **SHE** BE. WE FOUR BOYS WILL GO — NOBODY ELSE, AND THAT'S THAT!

Chapter 14

Tuesday evening at last

THERE WAS A MEETING THE NEXT MORNING TO TALK THINGS OVER ABOUT THE ARRANGEMENTS FOR TUESDAY. IT WAS A PROPER NOVEMBER DAY, AND A MIST HUNG EVERYWHERE...

MY FATHER SAYS THERE WILL BE A FOG BEFORE TOMORROW. IF SO THOSE FELLOWS ARE GOING TO BE LUCKY ON TUESDAY.

I DON'T EXPECT THE DRIVER WILL EVEN GUESS HIS TRAIN'S ON THE SIDE-LINE WHEN THE POINTS SEND HIM THERE! HE WON'T BE ABLE TO SEE A THING!

I WISH TUESDAY WOULD COME. SUSIE AND THE FAMOUS FIVE ARE JUST LONGING TO KNOW WHAT IT IS!

WON'T SHE BE WILD WHEN SHE KNOWS THAT IT WAS HER SILLY TRICK THAT PUT US ON TO THIS!

I MANAGED TO GET HOLD OF A RAILWAY MAP. IT SHOWS THE LINES FROM PETLINGTON AND ALL THE POINTS.

DO YOU THINK IT IT WAS A MAP LIKE THIS THAT ZEB AND LARRY WERE LOOKING AT IN TIGGER'S BARN?

IT MAY HAVE BEEN. I BET THOSE FELLOWS HAVE PLAYED THIS GAME BEFORE! OH, I DO WISH TUESDAY WOULD COME!

THEY HEARD THE SOUND OF A LORRY'S ENGINE THROBBING. VOICES CAME TO THEM, AND THEY SAW A LANTERN HELD BY SOMEONE...

THE GANG ARE HERE AND THE LORRY. YOU CAN JUST SEE IT OVER THERE. I BET IT'S GOT THE NAME HAMMOND OR DALLING ON IT.

IT WAS THIS TUESDAY. I DID HOPE WE HADN'T COME ALL THE WAY HERE IN THIS FOG FOR NOTHING!

Quietly, the boys found themselves a hiding place and settled down to wait. They knew they would be able to tell when a train was running over the main line some distance away because of the sudden explosions of the fog-signals, warning the drivers to look out for the proper signals or to go slowly. They had already heard two or three of the fog-signals going off on their way to the goods yard.

THEY WAITED... AND WAITED...

WHAT'S THE TIME?

IT'S ABOUT 6·30 NOW. THE 6·2 IS LATE BECAUSE OF THE FOG. IT MAY BE ALONG ANY TIME NOW, OR IT MAY BE LATER.

THEN — BANG! ANOTHER FOG SIGNAL WENT OFF AND THE BOYS WONDERED IF IT HAD GONE OFF UNDER THE WHEELS OF THE LATE GOODS TRAIN. IT HAD!

THE DRIVER CHECKED HIS SIGNAL AND WENT ON SLOWLY, NOT KNOWING HE WAS ON THE WRONG LINE!

LARRY WAS THERE AT THE POINTS, WELL-HIDDEN BY THE DARKNESS AND THE FOG, AND HE HAD SWITCHED THE GOODS TRAIN ON TO THE LITTLE SIDE-LINE...

THEN LARRY SWITCHED THE LEVERS AGAIN, SO THAT THE NEXT TRAIN WOULD GO SAFELY ON TO THE MAIN-LINE. HE DID NOT WANT HALF-A-DOZEN TRAINS ON THE SIDE-LINE TOGETHER!

THEN HE RAN DOWN THE SINGLE-LINE AFTER THE SLOW-MOVING TRAIN...

MOMENTS LATER...

IT'S COMING! I CAN HEAR IT. LET'S GO OVER THERE BY THAT SHED. WE CAN SEE EVERYTHING WITHOUT BEING SEEN. COME ON!

RUMBLE-RUMBLE-RUMBLE! THE GOODS TRAIN CAME NEARER. THE RED EYE OF A LAMP GLEAMED IN THE FOG. NOW WHAT WAS GOING TO HAPPEN?

Chapter 15
In the goods yard

FROM THEIR NEW HIDING PLACE THE BOYS COULD HEAR EVERY WORD THE THIEVES SPOKE...

WE'LL TELL THE DRIVER HE'S ON THE WRONG LINE. LARRY, YOU TELL HIM HE'D BETTER STAY HERE TILL THE FOG CLEARS AND HE CAN GET FRESH ORDERS.

I'LL TAKE HIM OFF TO THAT SHED AND HOT UP SOME TEA – KEEP HIM OCCUPIED WHILE WE DO THE JOB.

THE ENGINE-DRIVER IS JUMPING DOWN. HE'S LOST, I EXPECT!

THEY'RE GOING TO TELL THE ENGINE-DRIVER THAT HE'S RUN OFF THE MAIN LINE BY MISTAKE INTO THIS SIDE-LINE.

YES, AND THEN TAKE HIM OFF OUT OF THE WAY. THE GUARD TOO I EXPECT. AT LEAST THERE WON'T BE ANY FIGHTING.

HEY, YOU'RE ON THE SIDE-LINE! YOU OUGHT TO BE ON THE MAIN-LINE, RUNNING THROUGH THE STATION!

AY, I SHOULD BE. THERE MUST HAVE BEEN SOME MISTAKE AT THE POINTS. AM I SAFE HERE?

JUST THEN A FOG-SIGNAL WENT OFF JUST WHERE THE GANG WANTED THE TRAIN TO STOP. BANG!

THE ENGINE PULLED UP AT ONCE!

SAFE AS CAN BE! YOU'RE IN A GOODS YARD, BETTER NOT MOVE, THOUGH. THIS FOG'S TERRIBLE!

GOOD THING I GOT ONTO A SIDE-LINE!

JUST THEN, THE GUARD APPEARED...

SOMEONE MAKING A MESS OF THE POINTS NOW WE'LL BE HERE FOR THE NIGHT, AND MY MISSUS IS EXPECTING ME FOR SUPPER.

WELL, YOU MAY BE HOME FOR BREAKFAST IF THE FOG CLEARS!

COME ALONG TO THIS SHED. THERE'S AN OIL-STOVE THERE, AND WE'LL LIGHT UP AND HAVE A CUP OF SOMETHING HOT. DON'T YOU WORRY ABOUT TELEPHONING FOR ORDERS. I'LL DO THAT.

WHO ARE YOU?

I'M IN CHARGE OF THIS YARD. IT'S A BLESSING YOU GOT ON TO THIS SIDE-LINE. COME ON, LET'S GET SOME TEA!

THE MEN DISAPPEARED INTO THE SHED... AS PETER SAW FOR HIMSELF...

I EXPECT YOUR ORDERS WILL BE TO STAY HERE FOR THE NIGHT!

THEN THINGS MOVED QUICKLY. ZEB DISAPPEARED DOWN THE SIDE LINE TO LOOK FOR THE TRUCK COVERED BY THE TARPAULIN WITH WHITE MARKS — AND IN NO TIME HE WAS BACK...

IT'S THE SEVENTH TRUCK. COME ON, WE'LL START UP THE LORRY AND DRIVE IT DOWN.

CAUTIOUSLY, THE BOYS MOVED DOWN BEHIND THE LORRY...

DON'T YOU THINK WE OUGHT TO TELEPHONE THE POLICE?

YES, THERE'S A TELEPHONE IN THAT BUILDING OVER THERE. I NOTICED TELEPHONE WIRES GOING TO THE CHIMNEY THIS AFTERNOON!

THEY HAD TO CREEP PAST THE LORRY ON THE WAY, AND TO THE SURPRISE OF THE OTHERS, PETER STOPPED AND CLIMBED INTO THE CAB...

If You Want to Know the Time...

. . . Ask a policeman. But for many years you wouldn't have been able to find a policeman to ask! Instead, you would have had to have shared the duty of keeping 'The King's Peace'.

And it was not until after the Norman Invasion of 1066 that the old keeping the King's Peace system finally broke down. The conquering Normans, who had

little liking or sympathy for a people they did not understand, imposed their own fines and punishments. The British naturally resisted, and finally won the right to a more local system of law and justice. King John's signing of the Magna Carta was a natural development of this, and by the end of the 14th Century petty (or parish) constables had been installed.

They took an oath very similar to that our constables take today and their duty was to arrest criminals and other law-breakers. It was quite a popular system and in the country areas worked reasonably well, though unable to deal with a major revolt like that of Wat Tyler's in 1381.

It was very different in the large towns and cities, for those willing to become magistrates and watchmen were usually dishonest and out for their own ends. So much so that no honourable man would apply for these posts, and corruption was rife. Justice depended on the size of the bribes people could pay.

By the time of Charles II, although he tried to appoint Special Constables, known as Charlies, the maintenance of law and order had almost ceased to exist. The Charlies were just a joke to most citizens, whose boisterous sense of fun was by then pretty wild. It was not really until 1749, when the writer Henry Fielding was appointed magistrate at London's Bow Street, that the problem was seriously tackled again.

He was shocked by his findings. Hooliganism and violence were rampant, gangs of thugs (like the notorious 'Mohocks') roaming London's streets. One person in

every five of the population was possibly a criminal and life in general was held cheap.

So bad had the situation become and so menacing the cut-throats that Fielding was granted immediate financial aid to pay and organise a sturdy body of full-time constables, the Bow Street Runners. They were nicknamed 'Robin Redbreasts', for each wore a scarlet waistcoat beneath his blue frock-coat.

They carried a small hollow wooden baton known as a tip-

staff, a pair of handcuffs, and they were further armed with a pistol. The baton could be used as a truncheon or, in its hollow section, for carrying a warrant of arrest.

They proved tough, incorruptible and dogged enough to strike fear into the roughest of gangs. With Henry Fielding they were just the kind of Force London required.

The Runners were paid one guinea a week and, apart from their first duty to the Magistrate, could be hired for a guinea a day plus travelling expenses (up to fourteen shillings) by anyone requiring their services. Before long they were being called in by other authorities all over the country, their experience of London crime enabling them to make arrests where other forces had failed.

Several Runners have become famous and have gone down in history, as have some of their cases, the most well-known case being the Cato Street Conspiracy of 1820. In this they foiled an assassination attempt of all Cabinet members, the conspirators meaning to seize power by this plot.

A separate Police Force was enrolled for the City, and the Runners of Bow Street were enlarged by the formation of a mounted Horse Patrol in 1805. This put paid to almost all highway robberies, and the stage-coaches became a safer way of travel again.

In 1829 the Home Secretary, Sir Robert Peel, formed what was to be the start of the present Metropolitan Police Force, hence the old nickname 'Peelers'. They were first clad in white trousers, tail coats and top hats. The top hats not only served as a means of protection but could also be stood on in order to look over walls. They carried rattles for summoning help, these not being replaced by the familiar whistles until 1885.

Now the sight of a 'Bobby' or 'Peeler' prevented much London trouble and rowdyism, though it cannot be said they were popular with the public in general, there being a fear that personal liberty might be threatened by military control. Clashes between police and public quite often occurred and it took many years for Londoners to view the force with more sympathy and gratitude.

A particularly nasty murder in 1842 caused the formation of a regular detective force to be, for the first time, seriously considered. This kind of force was already in use on the Continent but for some reason had not been formed here. It was started rather cautiously and consisted of six Sergeants and two Inspectors only, their headquarters being attached to Scotland Yard.

What happened to these pioneers and what were their successes is not on record, it being likely they were not too successful. Things only changed when Chief Inspector Cavanagh arrived at Scotland Yard. He altered everything; the existing standards and general organisation. He had the gift of inspiring confidence in his men, encouraging them and getting the best from them. It would not be unfair to say that from his time the C.I.D. developed rapidly and became better established.

All in all, the foundations had been laid for the whole Police Force as we know it today.

Chapter 16

Hurrah for the Secret Seven

THE FOUR BOYS WERE SO EXCITED THAT THEY COULD NOT KEEP STILL. PETER FELT AS IF HE REALLY MUST GO AND SEE HOW THE GANG WAS GETTING ON BUT IN THE DARKNESS HE DIDN'T SEE THE MAN STANDING BESIDE THE LORRY...

OH!

HERE, WHO'S THIS?

YOU! THE KID WHO WAS ASKING QUESTIONS THE OTHER DAY! WHAT ARE YOU UP TO?

BUT THEN...

GRRRR!

AAAGH!

INSTANTLY, PETER AND SCAMPER VANISHED INTO THE DARKNESS...

WHAT'S THE MATTER? WHAT'S UP?

A BOY—AND A DOG! WE'D BETTER GET GOING. IS THE UNLOADING FINISHED? THAT KID MAY GIVE THE ALARM.

WHERE IS HE? WHY DIDN'T YOU HANG ON TO HIM?

THE DOG BIT ME, AND I HAD TO LET THE BOY GO. THEY'VE BOTH DISAPPEARED INTO THE FOG. COME ON, HURRY, I'VE GOT THE WIND UP NOW.

PETER HAD SHOT BACK TO THE OTHERS — PROUD OF SCAMPER'S ACTION!

GOOD BOY! BRAVE DOG! WELL DONE, SCAMPER!

75

I'LL WALK BACK WITH YOU. THERE'S NO ROOM IN THE CARS FOR ME NOW. BIT OF A SQUASH THERE AT THE MOMENT!

YOU SEE, WE'VE GOT OUR HANDS ON CHEEKY CHARLIE AT LAST. HE'S THE BOSS OF THE GANG THAT ROBS THE GOODS TRUCKS ALL OVER THE PLACE. A CLEVER FELLOW, BUT NOT QUITE AS CLEVER AS THE SECRET SEVEN!

THE INSPECTOR TOLD THE ENGINE-DRIVER TO REPORT WHAT HAD HAPPENED TO HIS HEADQUARTERS— THEN HE AND THE BOYS TRUDGED BACK TO PETER'S HOUSE . . .

WHAT HAVE THEY BEEN UP TO? A POLICEMAN HAS JUST BEEN ROUND COMPLAINING ABOUT THE CHILDREN TRESPASSING ON THE RAILWAY!

PETER'S CERTAINLY BEEN TRESPASSING ON THE RAILWAY AGAIN, BUT WHAT HE'S DONE THIS TIME IS TERRIBLY RIGHT. LET ME COME IN AND TELL YOU.

LATER, AFTER THE INSPECTOR HAD LEFT . . .

TOMORROW WE CALL A MEETING OF THE SECRET SEVEN — AND WE ASK THE FAMOUS FIVE TO COME ALONG TOO!

BUT WHY?

SO WE CAN TELL THEM HOW THE SECRET SEVEN MANAGE THEIR AFFAIRS! AND TO THANK THEM FOR PUTTING US ON THE TRACK OF THIS MOST EXCITING ADVENTURE!

HA! SUSIE WON'T LIKE THAT!

SHE CERTAINLY WON'T. FAMOUS FIVE INDEED! THIS WILL BE THE END OF THEM!

UP WITH THE SECRET SEVEN! HURRAH FOR US — HIP-HIP-HURRAH!

Answers to Nature Quiz

1 A Frenchman, noticing that the edges of the leaves were spiky or notched, decided they resembled the teeth of a lion and named the plant '*dent-de-lion*', from which our name comes.

2 Because the daisy opens early in the morning, our ancestors called it 'day's eye', this finally being shortened to 'daisy'. It was also called 'black-eyed Susan' because of the purple-brown, buttonlike centre.

3 Clover not only makes the soil very fertile but is also a valuable cattle food. Many farmers plant clover every few years.

4 Sunflowers can grow up to twelve feet tall and sometimes more!

5 All the fungus family (mushrooms, toadstools etc.) are without any greenery.

6 Moss usually grows on the northern side of tree-trunks, as the Red Indians discovered. From this they took direction.

7 'Rootstock' is the creeping, underground stem system of ferns.

8 Age is shown roughly by the number of rings on a cross-section of the tree's trunk, these being annual growth rings.

9 Sugar and syrup come from the treated sap of the Maple Tree, very important in North America.

10 Knotholes and knots are left when trees shed their own branches, this being Nature's way of encouraging fresh growth by 'pruning'.

11 By a rather elaborate process leaves produce a sugary fluid that feeds plants and trees.

12 and 13 Both are a means of attracting bees and insects needed by the plants for pollination—a plant's way of breeding. Without bees and other insects and birds there would be no fertilisation of flowers.

14 Geraniums.

15 Roses—some 5,000 varieties!

16 Trees have a single main trunk whereas shrubs divide into a number of stems from or near their base.

17 Broom and gorse.

18 The Sequoias (Californian Redwoods) can reach more than 300 feet high and be 2,000 years old. They were named after a famous Cherokee chief, Sequoyah.

19 With a little care and preparation almost all common trees can be grown (as dwarfs) in pots, but they will not flower unless transplanted out-of-doors in the normal way.

20 The Horse-Chestnut was introduced from the Balkans in Europe some four hundred years ago.

21 A grasshopper. The males produce a 'fiddling' sound by rubbing their wings together.

22 The hornet.

23 The dragonfly.

24 The web is spun of two kinds of silk, the spider carefully approaching along the non-sticky and non-elastic threads.

25 The spider can travel by its own parachute, making use of air currents etc. It actually steers the 'streamer'.

26 Moths generally sleep by day and fly only after dusk or at night, the very opposite to the butterfly.

27 The ladybird destroys most fruit pests (feeding off aphids etc.).

28 The mouth of a tortoise has saw-like edges.

29 An eel is a true fish, having both gills and fins.

30 The 'climbing perch'.

31 The wren. It is neither shy nor rare, just more difficult to see because of its size and swift movements.

32 The nightingale sings also by day, but other birdsongs make it less noticeable.

33 The approach of spring.

34 The robin.

35 A female blackbird is brown in colour.

36 It feeds on mistletoe berries and often sings in bad weather.

37 The raven is the largest of crows. It is an old legend that the Tower will fall if the ravens ever depart. So a 'Raven Master' at the Tower of London has the job of making sure this never happens.

38 One at the Tower was known to have lasted 44 years!

39 Ravens are scavengers and Londoners protected them for the service they did in this way.

40 The starling.

Peter is Janet's brother and the leader of the Secret Seven. The Seven meet in a shed in Peter and Janet's garden, and Peter makes sure they abide by the rules of the society, using the correct password and wearing their special badges. Peter is quick-witted and spirited, and is looked up to by the other members of the Seven.

Jack is brave and energetic and is really second in command of the Seven after Peter. He usually accompanies Peter on the more difficult and dangerous of the Secret Seven's adventures. He has a mischievous sister called Susie, who is not a member of the Seven, and who is always trying to ruin their plans!

Pam is a schoolfriend of Janet and Barbara. She is quite adventurous, but can be a little quarrelsome and stubborn sometimes!

Barbara is at school with Janet and Pam. She is a sensible and reliable member of the Seven, but is more timid than the other two girls.